HANG ON FOR DEAR LIFE!

Frank did his best to chase the intruder. He raced the snowmobile like a motorcycle, full throttle on every clear stretch and backing off at the very last moment on curves or through a jumble of saplings. The roar of the two machines shattered the quiet woods.

Joe, seated behind Frank, leaned closer and shouted, "We've got him!"

The intruder was only twenty yards ahead now. Frank saw the white oval of his face as he took a frantic glance back at them. Then the man swerved to the left, up a short slope.

Frank twisted the throttle all the way and followed. His quarry gained the crest of the slope and disappeared over the rise. An instant later Frank reached the crest and saw, just beyond it, nothing but open air!

"Aiee!" he shouted as the snowmobile became airborne like a ski jumper. Desperately tightening his grip on the handlebars, he glanced down into the shadowed depths of a rock-strewn ravine. . . .

Books in THE HARDY BOYS CASEFILES™ Series

Available from ARCHWAY Paperbacks

THE HARDY BOYS CASEFILES NO. 97

PURE EVIL

FRANKLIN W. DIXON

AN ARCHWAY PAPERBACK
Published by POCKET BOOKS
New York   London   Toronto   Sydney   Tokyo   Singapore

This book is a work of fiction. Names, characters, places and incidents are products of the author's imagination or are used fictitiously. Any resemblance to actual events or locales or persons, living or dead, is entirely coincidental.

AN ARCHWAY PAPERBACK *Original*

An Archway Paperback published by
POCKET BOOKS, a division of Simon & Schuster Inc.
1230 Avenue of the Americas, New York, NY 10020

Copyright © 1995 by Simon & Schuster Inc.
Produced by Mega-Books, Inc.

ISBN: 0-671-88208-2

First Archway Paperback printing March 1995

10 9 8 7 6 5 4 3 2 1

THE HARDY BOYS, AN ARCHWAY PAPERBACK and colophon are registered trademarks of Simon & Schuster Inc.

THE HARDY BOYS CASEFILES is a trademark of Simon & Schuster Inc.

Cover art by Brian Kotzky

Printed in the U.S.A.

IL 6+

PURE EVIL

Chapter

1

"HOW MUCH LONGER to New Hampshire, Frank?" Joe Hardy asked from the backseat of the van.

His older brother glanced at him in the rearview mirror. "We're nearly at the Vermont border," he replied. "Another hour, I guess. Anybody need a stretch?"

"I vote we keep going," Joe's girlfriend, Vanessa Bender, said. She sat forward in the seat beside Joe, her blue-gray eyes glittering with excitement. "I can't wait to see the farm where Callie's uncle Adam lives—it was great of him to invite us."

"You can't wait to do some cross-country skiing, that's what you mean," Joe teased.

"Okay, okay," Vanessa admitted. "That's a big part of it."

Callie Shaw turned around and smiled. "Adam is my great-uncle," she said, brushing back her blond hair. "And he didn't exactly invite us. *I* invited us. The truth is, I was surprised he agreed. Sapping season is the busiest time of year for him."

"I've always wanted to see how real maple syrup is made," Frank commented.

"From real maple trees," Vanessa joked.

"It's terrific stuff," Joe chimed in, smacking his lips. "I still remember the jug he sent you, Callie."

Callie nodded her agreement. "Uncle Adam makes the best syrup."

"You know what?" Joe continued. "When I go out skiing, I'm going to carry a little barrel of it around my neck, like a Saint Bernard dog—just in case I need to rescue myself."

They all laughed.

Just north of Brattleboro, Vermont, Frank left the Interstate for Route 5. Beyond a railway underpass, a green bridge led across the wide, lazy Connecticut River. Everybody cheered when they saw a sign that said Welcome to New Hampshire.

Soon they were driving through thick groves of evergreens. The branches were bent under the weight of the late winter snow, Frank noticed, and there was plenty of the white stuff on the ground, too. It looked as if they were in for some fine skiing.

Callie's great-uncle lived near the village of Waterboro, New Hampshire. Frank spotted a signpost and turned off the highway onto the village's main street.

It looked exactly the way a New England village was supposed to look. On one side of the tree-lined street was the Waterboro Inn, a white frame building with green shutters and a long front porch for summertime sitting and rocking. Across from it stood the church, town hall, a real estate office, and general store, which were all painted white and had green shutters, too.

Callie reached over and touched Frank's arm. "On through town, then make a left half a mile past the town pond," she said. "We're almost there."

Following her directions, Frank found himself turning onto a narrow dirt road between waist-high snowbanks left behind by a plow. On either side, rugged stone walls lined the road.

"That's it," Callie called out. "Shaw Farm."

Just ahead was a rambling two-story house with several huge old maple trees in front. A low passageway connected the house to a big red barn. Frank pulled into the driveway and parked beside a battered pickup.

"Hey," Joe said as the four climbed out of the van and stretched. "Is there a law around here that houses have to be white with green shutters?"

Before anybody could think of an answer,

Vanessa said, "Callie, there's an awful lot of smoke coming from that shack over there. Do you think there's a fire?"

Frank looked. Beyond the barn, at the edge of the woods, was a small, unpainted wood building with a metal chimney at one end and a sort of cupola that took up most of the roof. From openings in the cupola, dense clouds of white vapor were pouring out.

Callie laughed. "No, that's Uncle Adam's sugarhouse. And *that's* Uncle Adam."

Frank glanced at the man who was marching toward them. He wore a forest green jacket and green work pants tucked into high leather work boots. A red checked wool cap with earflaps partially covered his steel gray hair.

He nodded to Callie. "You're just in time."

"Hi, Uncle Adam. It's great to see you again," Callie said, giving him a kiss on the cheek. "Meet my friends—Vanessa, Frank, and Joe."

Adam nodded again, then said, "We'd best get started."

"Great," Joe said, with a broad smile. "I'll get the skis down."

"That can wait," Adam told him. "When the sap's running, sugaring comes first."

"Callie says you make the best maple syrup in the world," Frank said politely. "Can we watch?"

"You can do a sight more than watch," the

4

older man said with a hint of a smile. "Come along, the four of you."

He turned on his heel and marched back toward the sugarhouse. Near the door he stopped to point at a tall stack of split logs. "The fire never goes out when we're sugaring off," he said. "And you need logs to keep the fire going. Got to keep the sap boiling to evaporate the water in it."

"How do you get the sap?" Frank asked.

"In the old days, we used to hang buckets on all the trees," Adam replied. "Now I've got a system of plastic pipes that runs all over my sugar bush—that's what you call my forest." He pointed to an enormous grove of maple trees. "The sap goes straight from the tree through the tubing and into big barrels. Then I haul it here with a tractor and sled, and keep it in a holding tank until it's time to put it in the evaporator."

"A lot goes into this," Frank commented as he ran a hand through his thick brown hair.

"A lot of hard work," Adam agreed. He wrinkled up his face and glared at the four of them. "Don't know if city people are up to it."

"Oh, we're up to it," Joe assured him.

"Huh. We'll see," Adam retorted.

"You don't know Frank and Joe Hardy." Callie laughed. "The two of them can do almost anything once they set their minds to it."

Adam raised his eyebrows but didn't say anything.

They followed him into the sugarhouse. A bare light bulb dangled over a long, rectangular steel vat filled with bubbling sap. Frank thought the place was like a steam room.

Adam pointed to the cast-iron firebox door beneath the vat. "See that?" he said. "There's a good hot fire in there, all hardwood. Sap has to reach two hundred and twenty-one degrees before I jug it."

Callie moved to the other side of the vat. "Tell them how much sap it takes to make a gallon jug of syrup, Uncle Adam," she said.

"Forty gallons of sap to make one gallon of syrup," he said.

"Wow!" Joe said, his eyes wide. "That much?"

Adam nodded. "The sap's naturally sweet, but you have to boil it to concentrate the sugar. That's what the work is all about. Stay clear of the evaporator."

"You wouldn't last long if you fell in," Frank said, staring at the boiling sap.

"Or got pushed," Joe commented.

"You'd spoil my syrup, too," Adam added gruffly.

The door opened. A black-haired guy of about eighteen came in with an armful of split logs.

"Where have you been?" Adam demanded. "Didn't I say not to let the fire go untended?"

"You're here, aren't you?" the young man snapped back. He dropped the logs with a thud in front of the firebox door.

"This here is Bob Vale," Adam said. "He's my helper, or so they say."

Bob glared at Adam, then glanced at the four newcomers without saying hello. "I'll get more wood." He headed for the door.

"Kids these days don't know the meaning of hard work," Adam grumbled as the door shut behind Bob.

Callie caught Frank's eye and winked. "Oh, Uncle Adam, could we try your syrup?" she asked.

"Yeah, that'd be great," Joe said. "I'd love to taste it."

Adam scowled. "Never heard of such a thing," he said. "The rule is, work first, taste later."

"Oh, please," Callie pleaded again. "Just a sip?"

"No use trying to get around me, Callie," Adam said. "Still . . ."

As they crowded around him, he opened a drawer and took four tiny plastic cups off a stack. He filled each cup from the spigot of a stainless-steel container on a shelf near the vat.

"This is private stock," he added as he passed out the samples. "I collected the sap myself this morning from some special trees up back of the house."

7

"This is great!" Joe exclaimed after one taste.

"Fantastic," Frank said.

"Huh. Now let's see some fantastic work," Adam replied. He waited for them to finish their syrup, then started assigning chores. Frank and Joe were told to split logs and stack them behind the sugarhouse. Meanwhile, Vanessa and Callie's job was to shovel the heavy, wet spring snow off the path that led to the sugarhouse.

Bob stayed in the sugarhouse most of the time to watch the evaporator fire. When he did come out for more wood, he didn't say a word to anyone.

"What's with him?" Joe wondered as he watched Bob go back inside.

Frank shrugged. "Maybe he doesn't like outsiders interfering with his routine," he suggested. "Or maybe he doesn't like outsiders, period."

As Frank and Joe finished splitting the stack of logs, Callie and Vanessa rejoined them.

"I'm starved," Joe announced. "When's lunch?"

Adam came out of the sugarhouse in time to overhear. "When some of you city folk make it, that's when," he said. "Callie, how about you and Frank whipping up some sandwiches, while Joe and Vanessa take all your gear into the house?"

By the time the suitcases and skis were carried inside and put out of the way, lunch was ready. The big, plain wood kitchen table was loaded with a platter of Vermont cheddar and tomato sandwiches, a big bowl of tossed salad, glasses of milk, and a plate piled high with chocolate-chip cookies.

Adam turned on the radio. "You got to know the weather," he told them. "That's the most important thing in sugaring season."

"And now our forecast," the announcer said. "Tonight, clear with a low of twenty-three. Tomorrow, sunny with a high of forty."

Adam slapped the table with his palm. "Couldn't be better," he said.

"Why?" Frank asked.

"Cold night, warm day. That's what the maples need," he explained. "A cold night, the sap goes down into the roots. Then the next morning, the sun warms the trunk and the sap starts rising. If it don't flow up the trunk, it don't flow into my pipes and I'm out of the maple syrup business."

He left the radio on and sat down to eat.

"So do you think we earned some more syrup?" Joe asked. "Over ice cream or something?"

"Ice cream, with snow still on the ground?" Adam replied. "I never heard—"

"Listen!" Callie said suddenly.

From the radio, they heard, ". . . woman in serious condition with food poisoning. According to the police, the apparent source of the poisoning is a brand of maple syrup produced in Waterboro, New Hampshire—Shaw Farm Pure Maple Syrup."

Chapter

2

EVERYONE AROUND the kitchen table stared at the radio in disbelief.

The newscaster continued, "Stay tuned for the latest developments. Meanwhile, the police have issued an advisory. If you have recently bought any Shaw Farm Maple Syrup, do not use it until—"

Adam jumped up so quickly, his chair fell over backward. He gave the volume knob of the radio an angry twist. The radio crashed to the floor.

"Poisoned?" he shouted. *"My* syrup? Those fuzzy-brained bird-heads don't know what they're talking about!"

"There must be some mistake," Frank began. "Maybe—"

Adam turned and glared at him. "I'll tell you what the mistake is," he declared through clenched teeth. "It's listening to a lot of hot air coming out of that stupid little box."

The telephone rang. Adam answered it, then growled into the phone, "Sure, it's Adam Shaw. Who else would it be?"

His eyes narrowed as he listened. "You've got it all wrong, just like the fella on the radio. And I don't give a hoot what newspaper you work for," he bellowed, then slammed down the receiver.

"Who was that?" Frank asked cautiously.

"Some dim-witted reporter. Wanted to know what I put in my syrup." Adam shook his head.

Just then the old black rotary phone rang again. Adam stared at it. "I oughta pull the cord out of the wall," he threatened.

"Don't do that," Callie said.

"Then you answer it," he told her. "And if it's another snoop like the last one, tell him I'm dead." With that he stormed out the back door, slamming it behind him.

It was another reporter. Callie told the woman her uncle wasn't home and then hung up, visibly upset. "This can't be happening," she said. "Uncle Adam doesn't make bad syrup. He's as careful as possible; everybody knows that."

"Maybe somebody's got the facts all wrong," Frank said.

"There could be another syrup maker with the

same brand name," Joe suggested. "Or one that sounds like it."

Callie shook her head.

"The woman must have gotten sick from something else," Vanessa stated.

"I hope so," Frank replied. "But from what we heard on the radio, it sounds like officials analyzed the syrup and found something."

"But what?" Vanessa challenged.

He shrugged. "I have no idea. I just don't think the police would mention Shaw Farm unless they had some pretty convincing facts."

Everyone helped clear the table, then Joe washed the dishes while Vanessa dried. Callie and Frank put things away. They were finishing the job when they heard Adam in the front yard shouting at someone.

"Uh-oh," Frank muttered. "That sounds like trouble."

The four went outside and circled the house. Adam was standing in the driveway, bellowing at a gruff-looking, gray-haired man in a green plaid jacket. The man was shouting back.

"That's Karl French," Callie told the others. "He lives on the next farm over."

"He doesn't look very neighborly," Joe remarked.

"Karl makes maple syrup, too," Callie said. "He and Uncle Adam are huge rivals. They're always at each other. Can you believe it? They've been living next to each other their whole lives!"

As they approached, Karl shouted, "You finally found out you couldn't make a half-decent syrup yourself, so you decided to ruin the business for all of us."

"That's the most dumbbell thing I've heard since the time you tried to bribe the maple syrup judges at the state fair," Adam shouted back.

Karl moved forward until his nose was nearly touching Adam's. "Bribe them?" he roared. "Why, you worn-out sap bucket, the only way you won that ribbon was by stealing sap from my sugar bush."

"You'll do anything to steal my customers," Adam shouted. "Anything! And you know what I'm talking about, you toad-faced turnip-head."

"I don't have the slightest idea what you're talking about because *you* don't have the slightest idea what you're talking about," Karl replied.

"Then how come you're trespassing on my property again?" Adam demanded, jabbing a gnarled finger at his neighbor's chest.

"I heard the news reports," Karl said.

"You wanted to gloat, huh?" Adam said. "Couldn't wait to grab my customers?"

"No," Karl countered. "I tried to call you, but your line was busy."

Adam took a step backward. "Oh. Well, the next time you come sneak-thieving over here, trespassing and gloating about some dirty-dealing scandal that you created yourself, somebody is going to find you facedown in my evaporator."

Out of the corner of his eye, Frank noticed Bob standing beside the sugarhouse, listening. Bob saw Frank looking at him and quickly moved back out of sight.

That's funny, Frank thought with a frown. What's Bob got to hide? Or does he just want to avoid Adam?

Joe turned to Callie. "Could Karl have poisoned your uncle's syrup?" he asked in a low voice.

"I can't imagine it," she whispered. "They argue like this all the time, but that's about as far as it goes."

"But it's possible?" Frank pressed her.

Callie shrugged. "I guess so."

Vanessa was starting to say something, when three cars came speeding and bouncing up the road.

Frank watched as the cars swerved into the driveway and slid to a halt near the Hardys' van. Two men jumped out of the first car, one armed with a cassette recorder and the other with a thirty-five-millimeter camera. The second and third cars contained television news crews, who struggled to get their video cameras and microphones ready.

"Now look what you did, you old, chewed-up

wad of bubble gum," Adam shouted at Karl. "You told them to invade my property!"

"Me?" Karl shot back. "It's not my syrup that's poisoned. It's yours, you two-legged pile of sawdust."

Frank caught Joe's eye and smiled. He couldn't believe the way the two old guys were acting. They kept right on trading insults, never letting the other get the last word and paying absolutely no attention to the fact that the news crews were taping the whole scene.

The man with the tape recorder moved in closer. "Mr. Shaw?" he said. "Have you ever had problems with tainted syrup before?"

" 'Course not," Adam declared, turning to face the reporter. "It's all a bunch of baloney."

A woman in a trench coat and colorful scarf was holding a microphone. "Are you aware that twenty people have now been hospitalized, and that they all ate at the Hotcake House yesterday?"

"Who says?" Adam thundered back.

"The latest emergency room reports," the woman told him. "And the police. Is it true that the Hotcake House gets its syrup from you?"

Adam said nothing, but Frank knew his silence meant yes.

"They opened a new batch yesterday and served it to their customers," the woman continued. "The people who ate it got sick. The ones who didn't are fine."

"What? Ridiculous," Adam said, glowering at the reporter. "Bunch of groundless rumors. Somebody is trying to ruin my business."

Frank turned to Callie. "Who's that woman; do you know?" he asked quietly.

"That's Connie Page," Callie replied. "She has a morning news show, and sometimes she does the evening news, too. She's a very big name around here."

"Mr. Shaw?" the television newscaster continued. "Have you hired a lawyer?"

"What for?" Adam growled back.

"For your defense," she replied.

"I don't need a defense. Now, get off my property or you're the ones who'll need a defense." He took two steps toward the tight circle of reporters.

"Just one more question," Connie Page said loudly. "Will you be closing down your sugaring operation?"

"Why should I do that?" Adam demanded.

"Don't you care about what happens to the people who eat your syrup?" she continued.

"Nothing's happened to them," he retorted.

Another television reporter moved in. "Then how do you explain the twenty people hospitalized after eating your syrup?"

He doesn't have to explain anything, Frank thought. But he could tell that Adam was the kind of man who'd never back away from a fight.

"And what about all the people who don't yet know it's poisoned?" another reporter asked.

"It's not poisoned!" Adam shouted, waving his clenched fists in the air. "Now, get out of my way and off my land!"

"Don't you have any explanation?" Connie Page demanded.

"Sure I do," Adam declared. He turned and pointed at Karl French. "That polecat's behind it."

The reporters and camerapeople swung around almost like a single living creature with a dozen eyes. They focused on Adam's scowling neighbor.

When the news mob moved in on Karl, the Hardys rushed forward to rescue Adam from the frantic commotion. Without a word, Frank signaled for him to hurry to the house while he had the chance.

When they were halfway there, a burly cameraman looked back and called out, "Hey, Mr. Shaw, where are you going?"

The other newspeople spun around.

Adam ignored them and kept walking toward the house, with Callie and Vanessa leading the way and the Hardys behind him. The cameraman ran in front of Adam and began filming. Then a crew member from a rival television station tried to shove him aside. Adam walked straight at them, as if they weren't there at all.

Frank took a deep breath. This scene could get ugly—fast.

Just then, Connie Page pushed through the crowd and said to Adam, "Do you know who was among the people poisoned by your maple syrup yesterday at the Hotcake House?"

Adam stopped short and glared at her.

"Arthur Ellor, the president of CBN-TV," Connie Page continued. "Any comment?"

"Ayuh," Adam replied. "Maybe he deserved it if he puts up with the likes of you."

Frank saw the newspaper reporters scribble down the quote. The cameraman next to Frank asked a soundwoman if she'd gotten the words on tape. Frank groaned inwardly. The whole scene was turning into a ridiculous circus.

"Do you still say you had nothing to do with it?" Connie Page persisted.

Adam's face reddened. Jaw clenched, he turned on the crowd and grabbed a video camera from the nearest television crew member. The man was too startled to move, but the other camerapeople kept videotaping the action.

Adam marched toward the sugarhouse and stopped next to one of the sap barrels. Holding the expensive camera in both hands, he knocked the lid off the barrel with his elbow. Then he slowly lifted the camera and held it directly over the open barrel.

With an angry roar, the burly cameraman burst past Frank and Joe and ran headlong across the yard, straight at Adam.

Chapter

3

As THE FURIOUS CAMERAMAN got closer to Adam, the Hardys sprang into action. Frank jumped in front of him, crouching like a defensive lineman. The cameraman crashed into him, trying to push Frank out of the way. But Joe grabbed one of the man's arms and twisted it up behind his back.

"Arrgh!" the man cried. "Let go of me! That crazy old coot has my camera."

"Just take it easy, buddy," Joe told him. "We don't want anybody to get hurt, do we?"

The crowd of newspeople rushed over to photograph and videotape the conflict. As they came closer, Adam scowled at the immobilized cameraman and lifted the video camera higher.

"You're all a bunch of bloodsucking buzzards," he said. Then, as Frank watched in disbelief, Adam calmly released the camera. It splashed into the sap barrel and sank out of sight.

"There." Adam smiled smugly. "Go fish." With that, the older man started toward the house again. This time the mob of reporters and camerapeople didn't budge.

Callie was waiting by the front door.

"Callie," Adam shouted. "Go get Mr. Blunderbuss, quick!"

Who's Blunderbuss? Frank wondered. By the look on Callie's face, she herself wasn't sure what to do.

"Go on, girl!" her uncle shouted.

Callie disappeared into the farmhouse.

"Get off my property, all of you. I'm telling you for the last time," Adam hollered.

Nobody moved.

Callie came running back with a long-barreled colonial flintlock in her hands. Frank wanted to grab the antique gun away from her before the situation got worse. But she looked directly at him and gave a tiny nod of reassurance. She was trying to tell him that the gun wasn't loaded.

I sure hope she's right, Frank thought.

Callie handed the gun to Adam. The crowd began to back away, though the camerapeople and photographers kept taping and snapping photos.

Adam held the rifle diagonally across his chest. "Now, get out of here," he growled. "Before Mr. Blunderbuss here decides to join the discussion."

"Hey, calm down, old-timer," Connie Page said, backing up with the others. "We're going."

The newspeople sped off, leaving a stink of car exhaust behind them. Adam stood on his porch and watched, then went inside.

Frank and Joe followed him into the kitchen. Adam leaned against the sink, a baffled look on his face.

"Poison," he said, shaking his head. "Why in tarnation would I poison my own good syrup?"

"It's obviously a mistake of some kind," Frank said. "Here, let me put that rifle back up over the mantel."

" 'Tain't a rifle; it's a smooth-barreled musket," Adam told him. "And I'm hanging on to it. If those hyenas—or anybody else, including that noodle-head neighbor of mine—come back, I'll have this blunderbuss sticking down their throats before they know which way's up."

He lifted the gun by the barrel and pounded the heel of the wooden stock on the floor. Now Frank was doubly glad the gun wasn't loaded. Handling it like that might well have made it go off.

"Take it easy, Uncle Adam," Callie told him. "Just ignore them."

"How can I?" he demanded. "This is my business. Sugaring's my way of life. And those fools are ruining my reputation."

"They won't come back," Frank said.

"Frank's right," Vanessa added. "They got the message."

Adam scowled, then stomped across the kitchen and slammed the blunderbuss into the corner next to the back door. "It stays right here, in case I need it!"

"Does anybody want to go for a walk or something?" Vanessa asked, obviously trying to defuse the tension.

"No!" Adam said. He went back across the kitchen to the black cast-iron stove and picked up two small oak logs from the woodbox next to it. He pulled open the heavy stove door and shoved in the fresh fuel. After slamming the door closed, he turned and said, "That stove would be a good place for Karl—he'd do anything to ruin my business. He hates me, because my maple syrup's better than his and I sell more of it."

For the next few minutes Adam went on and on about Karl French.

Frank only half-listened to Adam's ranting. He was too busy thinking over the question of motive. Did Karl have big money problems? he wondered.

"And anyway," Adam added, turning away, "who'd be fool enough to trust a man who keeps a wolf as a pet?"

"A wolf?" Joe asked, his eyes wide. "A real wolf? I'd love to see that."

"Huh," Adam snorted. "I've seen it prowling around the woods. Karl French-fry feeds it, keeps it around, wants to make a pet of it. That's the kind of man he is."

He took a dented saucepan to the sink, filled it with water, and set it on the stove top.

"Do you want me to make some tea, Uncle Adam?" Callie asked.

"Nope," Adam said. "I'm just putting some humidity back into the air. Winter's dry, you know. We can't have you youngsters turning into shriveled old prunes like me."

Frank grinned. Despite Adam Shaw's gruff manner, he found himself liking the old man. He glanced at Joe. "I think we're going to have to investigate."

"You bet," Joe agreed quickly. "Don't worry, Adam, we'll find out what's going on and who's behind it."

"We'll all help," Callie told her uncle.

Adam gave a grunt, then said, "I don't need help. I already know who's behind it—that mean-eyed wolf lover next door."

"What if nobody did it?" Frank suggested.

"Nobody?" Adam asked, shoving the saucepan to the center of the stove.

"It could have been an accident of some kind," Frank explained. He shrugged. "We can't even guess until we find out the results of the lab tests. With so many people hospitalized now, the police are sure to conduct tests on the stomach contents of the victims."

"Right," Joe added. "Let's check that out first."

"But we still have to deal with the fact that the police think they've traced the poison to Uncle Adam's syrup," Callie reminded them.

"What?" Adam shouted, his face reddening again. "What's there to trace? Nothing. The only thing to trace is the slanderous lies Karl Fish Head has been telling about me."

Frank looked at Callie and shrugged slightly. It was obvious that Adam was going to explode whenever anyone mentioned the word "poison" in the same breath with his syrup.

The old man's growling subsided to a mutter.

"Er . . ." Joe said, hesitating. "What about the equipment? Could something have happened to cause an accidental impurity in the syrup?"

"What?" Adam shouted. "What did you say? There wasn't any accident and there wasn't any impurity. My equipment is perfect; my sap is clean; my syrup is pure. I sterilize the jugs, boil the sap hot enough, filter the syrup, watch every step of this operation. Nothing gets into my syrup that I don't know about. Nothing!"

"But you're not the only one who processes the syrup," Joe pointed out.

"What about Bob, Uncle Adam?" Callie said. "He could have made a mistake of some kind."

Before Frank could say anything, Vanessa added, "And maybe he was afraid to admit it. I know *I* would be."

Adam glared at her. "Afraid of what, young lady?" he asked.

Callie came to Vanessa's rescue. "Of you, Uncle Adam," she said as gently as she could.

Adam acted as if he hadn't heard her. "Bob? No way he could have made a mistake, because he does exactly what I tell him."

Frank wasn't so sure.

Suddenly the group heard a fast *thump thump* sound overhead. It grew louder and louder. Adam looked up at the ceiling, as if he had just developed X-ray vision. Then he rushed toward the back door, grabbing the musket on his way. Frank and the others looked at each other, then followed him.

A whirling helicopter was hovering in midair over the sugarhouse. The giant blades whipped a frigid wind through the trees, stirring up a blinding cloud of powdery snow.

"This is crazy," Joe shouted over the roar of the engine. "What does that guy think he's doing?"

Overhead, a cameraman stuck his camera out the side window of the helicopter and aimed it at Adam, who was shaking his fist. Then the angry farmer raised his blunderbuss and pointed it at the invading helicopter.

The camera was hurriedly pulled inside. Then the helicopter rose abruptly and sped away over the trees and out of sight.

Frank was just taking a deep breath when two cars came speeding up the dirt road and made a skidding turn into the driveway. One of the vehicles was a black-and-white police cruiser with a flashing light on its roof. It slid to a stop and the doors flew open. Two uniformed officers tumbled out and took cover behind the opened doors.

The second car stopped behind the cruiser, and an amplified voice boomed out, "Adam, this is Chief O'Brien. Put down the gun. This thing's gone far enough. We've got a warrant to serve on you."

Chapter

4

ADAM STOOD STOCK-STILL between the farm-house and sugarhouse, holding the ancient musket pointed at the sky. With his weapon and fierce expression, Frank thought Adam looked like the picture of the colonial soldier on a U.S. savings bond.

"He's going to get himself shot if he's not careful," Joe whispered to Frank. But to his surprise, the two police officers stayed crouched behind their car doors and did not draw their revolvers.

A white-haired man in khaki trousers and a navy blue parka got out of the unmarked car behind the cruiser. He began walking up the driveway toward Adam.

"That's Chief O'Brien," Callie whispered.

"Adam Shaw," the police chief called out. "Just what do you think you're doing?"

"Keeping the buzzards away," Adam answered in his loud voice, not budging an inch. "Whose side are *you* on, Mike—mine, or theirs?"

"I'm on the side of the law, Adam, and always have been," the chief replied. "Now, what's that thing you're holding, Adam?"

"If you don't know, you got no business pretending to be a cop," Adam said. "Why don't you just get back in your car and try to remember where reverse is?"

"You listen to me, Adam Shaw," the chief said. "I've known you all my life, and I never heard of you pulling the trigger on anything more than a varmint or two. So I'm coming up there and doing what I came here to do."

The police chief started walking slowly up the drive toward Adam. Callie's great-uncle let O'Brien get halfway to him, then he lowered the musket to the ground.

"That thing isn't loaded, is it?" the police chief asked, with a faint smile. "I hope not, for your sake. If you tried to fire it, you'd likely blow your hand off."

"Loaded?" Adam barely returned the smile. "What with? They haven't made bullets for this since the days when the Minutemen melted down their pewter plates and went off to Boston to hunt redcoats."

Relieved, Frank, Joe, Callie, and Vanessa crowded around Adam, who introduced them to Chief O'Brien. A moment later, a short man with a carefully trimmed mustache climbed out of the chief's car and hurried up the drive to join them.

"This is Mr. Maas, from the Health Department lab in Concord," the chief said.

"He's wasting his time here," Adam growled. "I'm not sick."

"A lot of other people are, Mr. Shaw," Maas said.

"We'll get to that presently," Chief O'Brien said. "But first, Adam, I got to tell you that the next time I hear you've been threatening people with that thunderstick of yours, I'm going to have to arrest you. Loaded or unloaded. You hear?"

"Is that what brought you out here?" Adam demanded. "I bet Karl Fish Head called to snitch on me."

Frank and Joe exchanged worried glances. Was Adam *trying* to get himself arrested? That's what would happen if the old man kept it up.

"It's got nothing to do with Karl French," O'Brien said. He reached to the inside pocket of his parka and pulled out a folded document. "Adam, I'm sorry as can be about this. But I've got a legal order here to close down your sugarhouse and impound most of your stock."

Adam stared at the piece of paper.

29

"It's all in order," Chief O'Brien said, trying to hand Adam the warrant.

Adam pushed it away. "In order? Whose order?" he demanded, his face taut and angry.

"Judge Bellows," the chief told him.

"Huh," Adam said. "Everybody knows that his mother's best friend was first cousin to Fritter French's pa."

"If I remember correctly, she was also *your* mother's cousin," O'Brien remarked.

Adam scowled. "That's neither here nor there," he said. "Rafe Bellows never thought this up himself. Who did?"

Gerald Maas stepped forward. "I did," he said. "I have a duty to protect the health of the public. And it's the duty of the police to assist me in doing it. Chief?"

Chief O'Brien beckoned to his two uniformed officers. When they hurried up, he said, "String a barrier ribbon around the sugarhouse."

"You can't do that!" Adam exclaimed. But as the two officers ran the line of yellow plastic around the shack, he watched quietly.

Too quietly, Frank thought. It was the calm of a steam boiler with its safety valve tied down.

"No one at all is to cross that barrier," Chief O'Brien explained. "Is that clear?"

"But, Chief," Frank said, pointing to the sugarhouse chimney. "The fire's still going. Shouldn't we put it out?"

30

"It'll burn itself out," the chief replied.

"What if it burns the sugarhouse down?" Joe demanded. "Will the town pay to rebuild it?"

"It won't burn down," the chief said. He called to his officer. "Did you check to see if anybody is in there?"

The officer said no.

"Well, do it," the chief ordered.

"He's not in there," Adam said.

O'Brien frowned. "Who isn't?"

"Bob Vale, my helper," Adam replied. "He's up in the sugar bush someplace."

Frank remembered Adam telling Bob never to leave the evaporator fire untended. Was Bob being careless, or disregarding Adam's orders? He made a mental note to try to find out later. Then he turned to Gerald Maas.

"What did you find in Adam's syrup that calls for such drastic measures?" he asked.

"Our investigations aren't completed yet," Maas said, looking uneasy under the unfriendly stares of Adam and the others. "We're still trying to sort out the problem."

Frank's eyes widened in disbelief. "You're closing down Adam's most important source of income at the most important time of the year, and you're still trying to sort out the problem? That's pretty irregular, isn't it?"

"You must have some kind of proof, to come and close down an operation like this," Joe said, stepping closer to Maas. "What is it? What did the laboratory find in the syrup?"

In spite of the late afternoon chill in the air, Frank saw drops of sweat on Maas's forehead. "It's not a question of lab results," he said weakly. "Every one of the victims ate Shaw Farm syrup. That's the only—and I mean *only*—common denominator. Some had pancakes; some had waffles; some had french toast. But they all had the poisoned syrup."

"Poisoned?" Adam shouted. He launched into a long speech about the purity of his syrup.

But Frank didn't pay much attention. He had just seen Bob Vale come out of the woods about a hundred feet away, notice the crowd, and duck back into the woods. Was Bob afraid of the police? he wondered. If so, why?

As Frank watched, Bob sidled toward the back end of the sugarhouse. He had a small red can in his hand. Head down and trying to look inconspicuous, he dropped the can into a tall trash barrel. Then he hurried out of sight behind the shed. What was he getting rid of?

As Adam rambled on, Maas took a step backward. "It's my duty to protect the public if something is potentially dangerous," he said when Adam stopped his tirade. "And in this case, it could very well be deadly."

"Did you find traces of anything harmful in the victims' stomachs?" Joe asked impatiently.

"Or in the syrup?" Frank demanded.

Maas looked over at Chief O'Brien. "Who are these kids?" he asked.

O'Brien shrugged.

Vanessa couldn't help herself. "Frank and Joe are well-known detectives," she said proudly. "They've solved a lot of difficult cases."

Maas raised an eyebrow in doubt. "Well, I don't have to answer their questions. All I can say is, the lab tests are still being conducted."

Chief O'Brien turned to Adam. "We'll be on our way now," he said. "But remember. That barrier means what it says—keep out. That goes for everybody. This is police business now."

Adam's lips were pressed together tightly as he watched the two men leave.

When they reached their car, the fury in Adam finally boiled over. He shouted after them, "That stack of logs knows more about what's happening than you two walking balloons. Can't you see? Karl French is outwitting you. He's the one behind all this. He's making eggshells out of everybody."

"Now, Adam," O'Brien said, pausing to look back. "I know you're upset."

"You couldn't find the Rocky Mountains in Colorado," Adam continued, ignoring him. "How can anybody expect you to find out that Karl French is pulling your chain right under your nose?"

"There's no evidence, Adam," the chief said, his voice rising to match Adam's.

Adam shoved the blunderbuss into Callie's hand and grabbed a gas can from the ground. He held it high in front of him and shouted, "If I blew up Karl's sugarhouse, I bet you two bat-eyed gumshoes wouldn't even notice the ashes!"

"Maybe not," O'Brien replied. "But if anything happens to Karl's sugarhouse, I suppose I know who to come looking for."

Adam turned on his heel and marched toward the house.

"Uncle Adam, wait," Callie called as she and the others hurried after him. "Please promise to do what they say." She glanced at the others for support.

"She's right," Vanessa agreed.

"It's my sugarhouse," Adam said harshly. "I'll go in there when I want."

That would really start trouble, Frank thought. "I hope you won't want to go in there too soon," he said. "At least not until they take the barrier down. Don't worry, we'll find out what's behind all this. You'll see."

"Absolutely," Joe agreed. "We're going to get to the bottom of this."

"Come on," Callie said, taking her uncle's arm, "let's go inside and start dinner. "

"Great idea, Callie," Joe chimed in.

Adam let them lead him to the kitchen door.

But before the Hardys reached the granite block steps, Frank grabbed Joe's arm. "You go on," he told the girls and Adam. "We'll be right there."

When he and Joe were alone, he asked, "Did you see Bob?"

"Yeah, I saw him, all right," Joe replied.

"He threw something in the trash. I'd like to know what it was," Frank continued.

They crossed the clearing to the trash barrel and peered inside. "It's empty!" Frank exclaimed.

"I don't get it," Joe said, frowning. "He threw that can in there. I saw him. You saw him."

Frank stared into the trash barrel and started to say something. But at that moment, the woodland silence was broken by a powerful *whump!* The ground shook from the force of a huge explosion.

Frank and Joe looked at each other in shock. "That came from French's place!" Joe exclaimed.

Chapter

5

As THE VIBRATIONS from the explosion rocked
Adam's house, Callie and Vanessa rushed to the
kitchen door.

"Frank, what was that?" Callie cried. "What
happened?"

"Something exploded," Frank replied. "Over
at Karl French's farm, I think. I don't know
what."

"Come on," Joe said. "We'd better go investigate. Somebody might be hurt."

Adam sauntered out onto the porch and leaned
on the railing. "Save yourselves the trouble," he
said. "That's just old Karl Fish-head, dynamiting
dead trunk stumps. I can tell by the sound."

"Now?" Frank asked, puzzled. "Why would he

36

do that while the ground's still frozen? Why not wait until the thaw?"

"Because that banana brain likes to get on my nerves, that's why," Adam replied.

"Isn't dynamiting dangerous?" Joe asked.

Adam smiled thinly. "I hope so."

"Uncle Adam!" Callie scolded.

Frank looked again in the direction of French's place, then he and Joe joined the others on the back porch. "By the way, where's Bob?" he asked Adam.

"Hither and yon," Adam replied vaguely.

"We saw him come out of the woods while O'Brien and Maas were here," Joe said. "He didn't seem to want them to see him."

Adam turned away. "Could be," he murmured. "Maybe the law gives him a rash."

"I noticed him throw something in that trash barrel by the shed," Frank said. "Any idea what it might have been?"

"Yup," Adam said with a nod. "Trash."

Vanessa laughed, then flashed Frank an apologetic look.

"When we looked in the barrel, there was nothing there," Joe stated. "I hope it wasn't an important clue."

Adam shrugged. "The dump's open today. Bob most likely made a run down there. It's one of his chores."

"The barrel's still where it was," Frank pointed out.

Adam gave a snort. "Oh, we're right up-to-date around here. We bag all our rubbish. It's the law, and good sense besides. Why truck a barrel when you can just lift out the liner bag? Say, what about that supper? All this ruckus has left me with a powerful appetite."

Joe and Vanessa volunteered to cook the meal. While Vanessa cleaned and sliced carrots and celery for an appetizer, Joe put a big kettle of water on the stove, then went to work on his famous two-alarm spaghetti sauce. Sliced garlic bread with herbs, toasted in the oven, completed the meal.

After eating, the group sprawled on the living room sofa and rug to watch the TV news. The first station featured interviews with some of the victims of the syrup poisoning.

One man looked straight into the camera and said, "I really thought I was going to die. I'll never eat maple syrup again." A moment later, the newscaster said that health officials had shut down Shaw Farm's sugaring operation and confiscated all jugs of his syrup from store shelves.

"That's enough," Adam said with a groan. "Switch the channel."

Frank pushed the arrow on the remote. Connie Page appeared on the screen, saying, ". . . and here's what we found." The picture changed.

There was Adam, surrounded by reporters, saying, "Poisoned? Maybe he deserved it." A moment later, two images of Adam holding the video camera over the sap barrel filled the screen.

This is bad, Joe thought. Very bad. Adam looked like a raving lunatic.

The reports got worse. The next picture was of the house and yard from a high angle. Adam came rushing out onto the porch, aiming his blunderbuss straight at the camera and the viewer. The screen went suddenly dark.

After a second, Connie Page came back on. With a grim face, she announced, "I want to assure our viewers that the news team here at Channel Six will not be stopped by vandalism, threats, and intimidation. Stay tuned for late-breaking developments. In the meantime, if you have any Shaw Farm maple syrup in your cupboard, the health authorities urge you not to use it until its safety has been established."

"I can't believe the way they edited the things you said," Callie said, putting a hand on her uncle's shoulder. "They made you seem totally guilty."

"It was a very slanted report," Frank said in agreement, snapping off the TV set. "But the only thing we can do about it is find out who's really to blame. Those people were poisoned, after all."

Joe nodded. "That's right. I say we get to

work, Frank. Let's stake out Karl's place and see what he's up to."

"I'm coming, too," Adam interjected. "Me and Mr. Blunderbuss."

"Oh, no, Uncle Adam," Callie quickly said. "That's not a good idea."

"Callie's right," Frank added. "If Karl spots you, he'll start blaming you for everything again."

"Besides," Joe said, "we need somebody here to back us up in case something goes wrong."

"Such as what?" Adam challenged.

Joe shrugged. "I don't know. Just in case."

Adam sniffed. "Don't think I can keep up with you, huh?" he growled.

"No, that's not it," Frank said soothingly. "We just don't want you to get into any more trouble."

Adam scowled, but sat back down.

Joe and Frank donned their parkas.

"Be careful," Callie warned.

"Make sure he doesn't think you're a couple of tree stumps and try to blow you up," Vanessa added.

In the dark, the Hardys followed Adam's directions up a dirt road that climbed the hill behind the sugarhouse. The road led through a gap in a stone wall onto Karl's land, then downhill several hundred yards to his sugarhouse. The lights were on and a snowmobile was parked to one side of the door. White smoke drifted from the chimney.

Frank motioned to Joe to follow him as they crept closer to the shed. They moved to the window and peeked in. Karl was standing on the far side of the big evaporator, his back to them.

"What's he doing?" Joe whispered. Frank touched his forefinger to his lips.

Karl half-turned. He was holding big test tubes in each hand, pouring the contents from one to the other. He raised the full one up toward the bare lightbulb, peering at it. Then he set the first test tube in a rack, reached for a jug of syrup, and poured the contents of the full tube into a jug.

When Karl took the jug toward the rear of the shed, Frank had to shift position to keep him in sight. As he did, he glanced backward. A shadowy figure was moving among the maple trees behind them. Frank peered into the darkness, trying to make out more details.

The figure hurried from one tree to the next. In the faint moonlight, Frank had the impression that the figure had something bulky on his back, and a stick or a spraying wand in his hand. What was he up to? Spraying something on the trees? Sabotaging the sap-collection system? Stealing sap?

Frank reached out and tapped Joe on the arm, then gestured toward the mysterious figure. Joe turned to look. His movement must have caught the attention of the intruder. The man remained motionless for a moment, then bent down and stood up again with something in his hands. As he raised it to his shoulder, Joe grabbed Frank's arm and pulled him to the snowy ground.

An instant later, there was a flash of flame and the crack of a hunting rifle. The bullet slammed into the wooden wall of the sugarhouse, just inches from where the Hardys had been standing. From inside, Karl gave a startled shout.

As Frank and Joe crawled quickly away from the pool of light cast by the sugarhouse window, Frank saw the rifleman run to a snowmobile half-hidden behind a tree.

"Try to head him off," Frank said quickly. "I'll take Karl's machine."

As Joe sprinted toward the trees, Frank ran to Karl's snowmobile and jumped into the saddle. The key was in the ignition. As the motor roared to life, so did that of the intruder's vehicle.

Behind Frank, the sugarhouse door slammed open.

"Stop, thief!" Karl shouted. "I'll get you for this!"

There was no time to explain. Frank gunned the motor and tore after the other snowmobile. Joe, knee-deep in snow, waved to his brother. Frank slowed down just long enough for Joe to jump on the back, then opened the throttle all the way.

The other guy had a sizable lead, but the Hardys could see the beam of his single headlight up ahead, illuminating the way, and they could follow the track of his snowmobile. As they raced through the maze of dark, thick maple trunks, turning and skidding, scraping through heart-stoppingly tight openings, Frank narrowed the gap between the two machines.

"Hold on!" Frank suddenly shouted to Joe. The snowmobile roared up one side of a snow-covered boulder and took to the air. Joe bounced off the seat. Only his desperate grip on the grab bars kept him from sailing off into the trees. A second later, the machine hit the ground, jarring his spine.

"You okay?" Frank demanded.

Joe leaned forward and shouted, "Fine. Go get him!"

Frank did his best, racing the snowmobile like a motorcycle, full throttle on every clear stretch and backing off at the very last moment on curves or through a jumble of saplings. The roar of the two machines shattered the quiet woods. Joe hit Frank's shoulder and shouted, "We've got him!"

The intruder was only twenty yards ahead now. Frank saw the white oval of his face as he threw a frantic glance back at them. Then the man swerved to the left, up a short slope. Frank twisted the throttle all the way and followed. Their quarry gained the crest of the slope and disappeared over the rise. An instant later, Frank reached the crest and saw, just beyond it . . . nothing but open air!

"Aiee!" he shouted, as the snowmobile became airborne like a ski jumper. Desperately tightening his grip on the handlebars, he glanced down, into the shadowed depths of a rock-strewn ravine.

The other bank of the ravine loomed up in the faint light. Frank wondered if they would survive the fall when the snowmobile crashed down on the steep slope. The engine screamed as the tread slipped in the deep snow. Then it caught, and the machine rocketed up the last few feet to level ground. Frank slid to a stop, just inches from a huge tree trunk, and took a deep breath.

"Joe!" He turned to look at his brother. "Are you all right?"

"Yeah, sure," Joe replied. "But I think my hair just turned white. What happened?"

"He suckered us," Frank said. "He must have made a sharp turn over the crest of the hill, knowing that we'd miss it. It's plain luck that we're not at the bottom of that ravine."

"With our snowmobile on top of us," Joe added. "What now?"

As if in answer, the other machine started up again. The man must have been waiting to see the results of his ploy.

"We chase him—what else?" Frank replied, gunning the engine.

As they followed the sound of the other snow-mobile, Frank noticed that they were angling steadily to the right. What was this? The guy was leading them right back toward Karl's sugarhouse!

Moments later, they were on the dirt road, with the lights of the sugarhouse at the foot of the hill. The intruder steered straight for the wooden shed, then skidded to a halt next to the side window. Frank saw the mysterious figure throw something through the window before roaring off into the darkness.

What was that? Frank thought.

"Frank, look!" Joe said urgently. "It's Adam!"

He was right. Callie's uncle was standing outside the sugarhouse, looking after the fleeing snowmobile with a baffled expression.

Suddenly Frank had a terrible feeling in his gut. "I know what that guy threw," he murmured. Then, standing up in the seat, he yelled, "Adam, run! It's a bomb!"

Chapter

6

ADAM STOOD next to the sugarhouse door, too stunned to move. Without a second's hesitation, Frank steered the snowmobile straight toward him, then swerved and cut the power.

Joe knew exactly what to do. As they came alongside Adam, he reached out, grabbed the wide-eyed farmer by the front of his jacket, and yanked him onto the saddle of the snowmobile, between him and Frank.

The engine howled as Frank twisted the throttle grip all the way open. A shower of snow shot up from behind the churning tread. Frank sped down the track, aiming for the shelter of the trees. Just as he reached them, a flash of white flame lit the dark woods. The explosion's roar drowned out the noise of the snow-mobile engine.

Frank stopped the machine. He, Joe, and Adam leapt off and looked back. The blast had blown out the door and windows and part of the roof of the sugarhouse. From inside, fierce orange flames were licking at what was left. Frank gave Joe a sober glance. No one inside could have possibly survived that explosion and the inferno it had created.

"Karl was in there," Joe said.

"Well," Adam replied in a shaky voice. "He was a crazy old coot and never made a decent drop of syrup in his life. All the same, I'm sorry to see anyone go like that."

The solemn silence was shattered by a shout from behind them. "You old villain, you! Trying to corner the market with your poisonous syrup by blowing up my sugarhouse? I ought to shoot you down, like the mad dog you are. You and those two pups with you."

Frank, Joe, and Adam whirled around. Karl French was just a couple of dozen feet away, with a rifle under his arm.

"No such thing," Adam countered. "Why should I bother to blow up your place? Everybody knows who makes the best syrup around here."

"Then what are you doing sneaking around on my land?" Karl demanded.

"I heard a shot and came over to find out what kind of dumb move you'd made this time," Adam retorted. "What're you doing here?"

"I live here, you two-legged turtle," Karl said. "And what about those two? They stole my snowmobile."

Relieved to find Karl alive, Frank quickly told him about the mysterious figure lurking around his maple trees. "He took a shot at us, then tried to escape on a snowmobile."

In the distance Frank heard the wail of sirens. He hoped that meant the fire department was on the way. "I'm sorry there wasn't time to ask permission," he told Karl. "We borrowed your machine so we could chase the guy. He led us back here and threw that bomb into your sugar-house. We were afraid you were still inside."

Karl shifted his rifle a little. "I can't think of one solitary reason to believe you," he said. "What were you doing snooping around my property in the dead of night?"

Before the Hardys could answer, Adam demanded, "What were *you* doing, this time of night?"

"What?" Karl shot back. "I was testing the grade of the syrup I was boiling."

Without thinking, Joe said, "So that's what those test tubes were for."

Karl gave him a narrow-eyed stare. "Spies!" he said. He turned to Adam. "I should have known it. You got them to spy for you, huh? I have half a mind to call the police and get you all arrested for trespassing."

"Half a mind?" Adam responded. "Well, you used up the other half a good ten years ago. So what's that leave you? Just enough to whomp up some kind of test tube poison for my syrup."

This time Karl didn't bother to reply. Instead he stared at his burning sugarhouse in silence. It was the first time in five minutes the two men had stopped arguing. In the fire's glowing light, Karl's face looked pale and solemn.

"Look, Mr. French," Frank said softly. "It wasn't Adam who blew up your sugarhouse. He was almost killed himself."

"It was that guy on the snowmobile," Joe added. "We saw him. He threw the bomb through the window and disappeared."

Karl turned to the Hardys. "Oh, yeah? What'd he look like?"

Frank shrugged. "It was too dark to get a good look," he admitted.

Karl pointed at Adam, his scowl returning. "It was probably that kid helper of his," he said. "What's his name? Doing a favor for his boss."

"Bob Vale?" Frank asked.

Adam harrumphed. "It was probably someone working for Karl. Skinflint here never paid him for poisoning my syrup, so he decided to turn the tables."

"What?" Karl shouted. "You old fool! That's the dumbest thing you've said in years, and that means *really* dumb!"

He turned to the Hardys. "You caught a glimpse of the guy. Come on, what did he look like?"

Frank shook his head. "He was too far away, and it was too dark," he told Karl again. "But here's what worries me. The light through the sugarhouse window was shining on us. This guy, whoever he is, can identify us. And he doesn't know that we can't identify him."

There was a silence, as the meaning of this sank in.

Suddenly several fire trucks, their sirens blaring, tore up the driveway. The firefighters jumped off and uncoiled their hoses. Ten minutes later the fire was out.

Callie and Vanessa ran toward the Hardys, each holding a powerful flashlight. "What happened?" Callie cried. "We saw flames and called the fire department."

"The whole sky over here was red," Vanessa added. "We were so worried."

Joe filled them in.

"On the way over, a snowmobile went by," Callie said. "I called out, but it just kept going."

"Did you see who was on it?" Frank demanded eagerly.

She shook her head. "No, sorry. I thought it must be Bob, on his way back from somewhere."

After the firefighters had left and Karl went inside the main house, Frank took Callie aside. "Would you take your uncle back to the house and make sure he stays out of trouble? We'll be back soon. Can we borrow one of your flashlights?"

"Sure," Callie told him. She went over to Adam and persuaded him to leave with her and Vanessa.

While Adam and the girls started for home, the Hardys walked into Karl's sugar bush. Frank glanced back at the charred remains of the sugarhouse, trying to gauge exactly where he had seen the shadowy figure.

"The guy was about here, I think," he said finally. He shone the flashlight up and down the trunk of the nearest maple tree. Three metal spouts were stuck through the bark to reach the sap layer. The blue plastic tubes that collected the sap looked untouched.

He and Joe circled the tree twice, looking for clues or something that seemed out of place. Then they moved on to the next tree, then the next.

Frank sighed. "It's hard to be sure in the dark. But I don't see any sign of tampering. Do you?"

"Nope." Joe shook his head. "But we don't know how long that guy was up here."

Frank nodded. "That's right. Maybe we spotted him before he had a chance to get started."

After a moment's thought, Joe said, "No, that can't be right. He had that snowmobile."

"Of course!" Frank replied. "If he'd come up while we were here, we would have heard the noise."

"And Karl, too," Joe pointed out. "He was in the sugarhouse."

"Right," Frank said. "So our culprit must have been hanging around here for quite a while. But why? What was he doing?"

"And why did he blow up Karl's sugarhouse?" Joe added. "Was that his plan all along? Or did he decide to do it after we started chasing him?"

Frank scowled in concentration. "When we first spotted him, he ran away, remember? It was only when he couldn't shake us that he circled back and threw that bomb. To me, that looks like he had the bomb along just as an emergency measure."

"And we provided the emergency," Joe said. After a short silence, he continued, "I'll bet Bob is a good snowmobiler. And he's bound to know his way around these woods."

Frank scratched his chin. "There's something a little strange about him, no question," he said.

"Adam gives him a hard time," Joe pointed out.

"Well, it worked on me," Frank admitted. Watch out, there's broken glass on the floor."

Joe bent down and found his slippers under the bed, then stepped into them. Frank did the same.

"There's a note tied to the brick," Frank pointed out. He took off the small square of paper and unfolded it.

" 'You couldn't catch me at Karl's,' " he read aloud, " 'and you won't catch me ever.' "

The Hardys looked at each other. Joe said, "We'll see about that."

"Do you know what this means?" Frank asked, then answered his own question. "The guy we were chasing this evening not only knows who we are—"

"But where we're staying." Joe finished his brother's thought. "How could he have known which window to throw this brick through?"

"Inside information?" Frank suggested. "Either that, or he was watching the house. Unfortunately the note's typewritten, so we can't trace the handwriting."

There was banging on the door of the room. "Hey, what's going on?" Callie called. "Are you guys okay?"

"We heard something break," Vanessa added, worry in her voice.

Joe opened the door. "Better not come in," he said. "There's broken glass on the floor."

Adam appeared in the hallway. "What's the

Frank laughed. "Adam gives *everybody* a hard time."

"Yeah. Well, how about this?" Joe continued. "Maybe Bob isn't the one who poisoned the syrup, but he's working for the guy who did. Remember how he stayed clear of the police? Maybe he listened to our conversation with Chief O'Brien, then tipped off someone that we were onto something."

"But why would Bob try to sabotage Adam?" Frank asked.

Joe replied, "To get even with Adam. Maybe he doesn't like being bossed around."

Frank shook his head. "That's much too flimsy. It's like saying that Vanessa is working for the other side because Adam didn't like her carrot and celery appetizer at dinner. Come on, we'd better get back. Maybe Karl will let us come back tomorrow and look around by daylight."

Back at the farmhouse, the Hardys shared cocoa and cookies with Callie and Vanessa and talked over the event-packed day.

"This isn't just about ruining Adam's business anymore," Vanessa remarked. "That bomb could easily have killed both Adam and Karl. That means we're up against a potential murderer."

There was silence as everyone took in her words.

Then Adam appeared in the doorway in a long red flannel nightshirt. "Can't a body get any rest around here?" he grumbled. "We rise with the chickens in these parts, you know. Go on, shoo!"

Frank and Joe said good night to the girls and went to their room at the back of the farmhouse. After such a long day, sleep came quickly.

But later in the night something awakened Joe. He sat up in bed, wondering what he'd heard. Then the noise came again. Somewhere in the forest, the sound of a snowmobile's engine revving disturbed the winter silence. It drew closer.

"Frank!" Joe whispered, reaching across the gap between the two beds to shake his brother's shoulder. "Frank, wake up!"

"Huh?" Frank said groggily. "What is it?"

A moment later, the window in the bedroom shattered, showering the Hardys with shards of broken glass. Something heavy crashed onto the wide pine floorboards.

"Look out, Frank," Joe screamed. *"It's another bomb!"*

Chapter

7

THE HARDYS LEAPT out of bed as if the she were on fire. Joe was a split second faster th his brother. He reached down and scooped the perilous package.

"Throw it out, quick!" Frank shouted, pu up the shattered window.

Joe cocked his arm like an NFL quarte As his arm came forward, he hesitated. it," he said.

"What?" Frank exclaimed. "Are you n it out of here!"

"Turn on the light," Joe said. Aft turned on the lamp, Joe held out the his hand. "Look. It's not a bomb at a a brick. Scare tactics."

ruckus?" he demanded. "Did somebody start World War Three?"

Frank and Joe explained what had happened and showed the others the brick.

"Just like old Karl, spoiling an honest man's sleep," Adam muttered. He stomped off down the hall and returned with a square of plywood, a hammer, and a glass jar of assorted nails. While Joe and Vanessa swept up the broken glass, Frank and Callie tacked the plywood over the shattered window to keep out the cold. Then all of them returned to their rooms and tried to get back to sleep.

At breakfast the next morning, Adam turned on the radio to hear the weather report. Instead, they heard a newscaster say that eight more people had been hospitalized for maple syrup poisoning.

"All of the new victims, like the earlier ones, were stricken after eating the Shaw Farm brand of maple syrup," the broadcaster finished.

Joe glanced over at Adam, expecting another outburst of fury. But the farmer was sitting in silence, twisting his hands together, his face pale and drawn.

That was just the start. All morning they heard bad news. Adam walked down to the road to pick up his newspaper and returned to display a front page with the headline "More Poisonings Linked to Shaw Farm Syrup."

"That's enough," Adam muttered. "No more lying radio, TV, or newspapers in this house."

Frank said, "But we need all the information we can get. If you don't feel up to watching or listening—"

"Hold on, son," Adam growled. "I can take anything they dish out. Callie? Turn on the set to Channel Six. It should be just about time for that overdressed, no-brain gal they have the nerve to call a reporter."

Callie found the remote and switched on the set. Connie Page appeared, saying, "My guest this morning is Jud Gagnon, a local man who's developed a genetically engineered maple syrup called Gagnon's Gold that will hit the market in the next few days. Mr. Gagnon, welcome to 'Good Morning, New Hampshire.' Tell me, what did you think when you heard all these news reports about poisonous maple syrup?"

Gagnon was a stocky man with dark hair and a thin mustache. "I was upset, Connie," he said. "But I can't say I was surprised. Let's face facts. Old-fashioned tree-made syrup, like this Shaw Farm brand, is obviously dangerous. Consumers should know that Gagnon's Gold is a completely different form of maple syrup that's safe because it's totally man-made."

"Why would that be any better?" Connie Page asked.

Gagnon smiled into the camera. "We've all heard about the dangers of acid rain," he said. "Apparently it has finally increased to a deadly level, especially if it's concentrated in syrup. Environmental scientists have proved that millions of tons of lethal chemicals are carried east by the jet stream across the country to New England. That's the direction the prevailing winds blow."

"What's in this acid rain?" Connie asked.

"Among other things, dangerous heavy metals—mercury and lead," Gagnon said. "Not to mention pesticides sprayed by airplanes on farms, and hydrocarbons from urban pollution. All this falls with the rain on our New Hampshire forests. Maple trees absorb these toxic substances through their leaves and roots, and pass them into the tree's sap. When the sap is boiled down and highly concentrated in the form of syrup, these trace chemicals can become potentially lethal to humans—as we've tragically seen."

"Can you believe this guy?" Joe demanded. "The authorities haven't even released information about the cause of the poisonings yet. How can he make all these claims?"

"He's trying to take advantage of Adam's bad luck," Frank replied. "He's using something everybody's heard of, like acid rain, and blowing it way out of proportion. Sure, it's a serious problem. But if it falls on maple trees, it falls on apple trees and potato plants and lettuce, too."

Then Connie Page asked Gagnon what he thought viewers should do.

Gagnon smiled at the talk show host. "We all love maple syrup," he said. "But anyone who wants to be safe should wait for my new artificial syrup. Gagnon's Gold is made in New Hampshire, but not from trees."

Adam sat without a word and stared at the screen.

The program continued with Connie Page interviewing a panel of environmentalists, biologists, and dendrologists, or tree specialists. Contrary to what Jud Gagnon had implied, the laboratory analyses showed that no foreign substances had been detected in Adam's syrup. The experts sounded baffled but agreed that something must be wrong with the syrup itself.

"Have any of you seen this kind of poisoning before?" Connie Page asked her panel of experts.

"Well, no," a biology professor admitted. "We must be dealing with some sort of mutant maple tree that yields toxic sap. When you boil it down to make syrup, the toxins get concentrated enough to hurt people."

"One last question," the newscaster said. "How do we deal with this terrible problem?"

A young woman from the state Board of Health answered. "Where the safety of the public is concerned, we have to err on the side of caution. If there's even a remote chance that those maple trees are producing some kind of toxic sap, there's only one answer. The authorities should go in and cut every one of them down."

Joe jumped to his feet. "What?" he shouted. "Did you hear that?"

"They can't do that!" Vanessa declared. Then, in a small voice, she added, "Can they?"

"If they get a court order, yes, I imagine they can," Frank told her.

"We've got to do something," Callie said.

"I'll do something," Adam proclaimed. He grabbed the power cord for the TV and yanked it from the socket. "There!"

An hour later, Frank glanced out the window. A bright red luxury sedan cruised into the driveway and stopped. A squat man with a round face climbed out, walked up to the front door, and knocked. Frank opened it.

"Hello there," the man said. "Is Adam around?"

Adam appeared from the kitchen with Joe right behind him. "Nick Unger," the old man said. "I should have expected to see you. Come buzzing around the carcass, have you?"

"You love to have your little joke, don't you, Adam?" Unger replied. "Fact is, I'm here to do you a good turn."

Adam gave Frank an ironic glance. "Here's a piece of good advice, son," he said. "When a real estate agent says he's out to do you a good turn, keep a firm hand on your wallet. And after he goes, be sure to count the spoons."

A hint of pink came into Unger's cheeks, but he kept on smiling. "Always the kidder," he said. "I admire that, Adam, I really do. Especially considering your troubles. That's why I came here to help."

"Get on with it," Adam said. "What do you want?"

"All right now, Adam," Unger said. "I know you're a man of few words. So I'm going to get right to the business at hand."

"Oh?" Adam growled. "When?"

Frank caught Joe's eye and smiled.

Unger looked disconcerted for a moment. Then he said, "Right now. I'm here to make you an offer for this fine property of yours."

Adam stared at him. "A *what?*"

"An offer. I'd like to buy this place," Unger said. "Listen, Adam. Now's the time to sell. All this talk about poisoning, and health hazards, and cutting down your sugar bush . . ." He paused, then put his hands in his pockets. "Better sell now, before all the talk drives the value of your property down to zero."

Adam stared at him, speechless.

Frank jumped in, asking, "If you're so sure the

value of this place is going to go down, why do *you* want to buy it?"

Unger smiled and straightened his tie. "I've always liked this place."

"But what about the poisoning?" Joe asked.

Unger fidgeted. "I'd be surprised if there was any truth to that," he said.

Adam took two steps in Unger's direction and stared at him, nose to nose. "You money-grubbing, two-legged hog," he seethed. "I wouldn't sell my land to you if I was starving and eating bark. Buy my place? You'll have to kill me first, and then sweet-talk my heirs!"

"Take it easy, Adam," Unger said, pasting a smile on his face. "I can tell you're upset. But think it over when you're feeling calmer. You won't get a friendlier offer, I guarantee."

Unger left, and Adam, Frank, and Joe went into the kitchen, where Callie and Vanessa were sitting at the table.

"Who is that guy?" Joe asked.

"He calls himself a developer," Adam told them. "He buys up land, builds cheap and ugly buildings, and takes off with the profits to ruin another town. He wants to do that to Waterboro, but so far the town selectmen have stopped him. Now he wants my farm for one of his schemes."

"And Karl's?" Joe asked.

Adam considered the question. "Wouldn't surprise me."

"Has he been after you to sell, Uncle Adam?" asked Callie.

"Nope. First time," Adam told her.

"Why didn't he try to buy it before?" Vanessa wondered aloud. "Do you suppose he was waiting for some crisis like this to come along?"

"Or planning to *create* a crisis?" Joe chimed in.

"I wouldn't put it past him," Adam grunted.

Suddenly, from somewhere up the hill, they heard the powerful whine of a chain saw.

Frank looked at Adam, who frowned and said, "That better not be from anywhere on my property, or some fathead's in big trouble."

"We'll go check it out," Frank promised.

He and Joe went outside and hurried up the hill toward the noise. In a clearing, three mean-looking, muscular men were attacking three huge maple trees with chain saws.

"Hey!" Joe yelled over the din of the saws.

The men looked up, surprised. Then, one by one, they pulled their saws from the trees.

Frank froze in his tracks as they advanced on the Hardys, their deadly blades buzzing.

Chapter

8

JOE AND FRANK STOOD shoulder to shoulder as the three menacing thugs stepped toward them, their chain saws raised at threatening angles.

Frank knew karate, but he was starting to wonder how much use it would be against a powerful chain saw. Suddenly the thug in the middle looked past Frank and Joe, and hesitated. His face grew snow white.

Frank risked a lightning glance over his shoulder. A fierce-looking, brownish gray dog had entered the clearing. It was staring at the three intruders with piercing eyes. A low growl came from its throat. When Frank turned back, he saw that the three hoods were slowly backing away.

As the animal paced silently past Frank and

Joe, it kept its gaze fixed on the three men. The fur on its back was raised, and its big white fangs were bared. It crouched low, its belly touching the ground.

It looks just like a wolf, Frank thought. Could it be Karl's pet?

The vicious-looking animal approached the three intruders, circling to the right. They continued to back away, herded toward the edge of the woods. Each one switched off his chain saw, as if hoping that would calm the animal.

As the thugs retreated, Frank noticed that the man nearest him had a triangular shoulder patch on the left sleeve of his green jacket. Frank narrowed his eyes and tried to make out what it said, but the man was already too far away.

Frank decided to risk a bluff. "Who sent you here?" he demanded. The wolf glanced at him, then continued to stalk the three thugs.

"Call off that beast," the man with the shoulder patch replied shakily.

Frank pressed his advantage. "Who told you to cut down these trees?" he demanded again.

One of the other men suddenly yanked the starter cord on his chain saw. The machine caught hold with a roar. The man aimed the whirring blade at the trunk of the nearest maple tree.

Instantly the wolf leapt toward the man, its jaws opened wide for a slashing attack. The man watched, frozen with fear.

Over the din of the chain saw, Joe shouted, *"Heel!"* To his amazement, the animal stopped the charge almost in midair. The wolf looked back at Joe as if waiting for his next command.

Joe turned to the three frightened men and said, "One word from me and he'll tear your throats out. Now—who sent you here?"

The men threw down their chain saws and ran into the woods. The wolf took off after them. Joe watched, amazed again. The wolf could have easily caught the men. Instead, he was staying just close enough to make sure that they ran away. It was as if he knew that his job was to protect the woods, not kill trespassers.

Joe turned to Frank and gave him a high five.

"What made you think of telling that wolf to heel?" Frank demanded.

"Beats me." Joe grinned. "But I'll tell you one thing. That can't be a purebred wolf, or it would never have stopped—no matter what I said. It's at least part dog, and Karl has done a fine job of training it."

Callie, Vanessa, and Adam hurried up behind them. Frank told them what had happened. Adam rushed to inspect the three trees, then straightened up with relief on his face.

"They're not hurt too badly," he said. "You got here just in time. Not only that, we got us three fine new chain saws—free of charge."

From behind them, Karl said, "So you finally

decided to turn this no-good sugar bush into planks for a bowling alley?"

"What're you doing on my land?" Adam asked.

"I was out cleaning up after the fire," Karl replied. "And my wolf took off on me. He headed up this way. Anybody seen him? And what's all this sawing going on?"

As Frank and Joe told him what had just happened, Karl's pet trotted into the clearing and came over to sniff Joe's hand.

"Is this really a wolf?" Joe asked, holding himself very still.

"Not really," Karl admitted. "He's a stray I adopted. I needed a watchdog, and I figured trespassers and such would respect him more if the word got around that he was a wolf."

Adam snorted. "Tricking people again?"

"He's close enough to a wolf for me or most folks," Karl retorted. "Looks as though he's taken a liking to you," he continued, turning to Joe. "No accounting for tastes, I reckon."

Frank told the two men about the shoulder patch on the thug's jacket. "It was sort of a triangle with curved sides," he explained. "Dark green with letters or a design in white. Does that mean anything to either of you?"

Karl and Adam glanced at each other and paused.

"Could be most anything," Karl said.

"State game wardens wear a shoulder patch on their jackets," Adam said. "But our local warden is off on another assignment up north. And I don't see him mixing in with something crooked."

"You know what I'm wondering?' Joe said. "That real estate agent—what's his name?"

Adam spat, then said, "Nick Unger."

"How does Nick Unger fit into all this?" Joe continued.

Adam made a noise of disgust. "He can go fit himself into a drain pipe, for all I care."

Joe grinned, then continued. "But what if, after he left your place—"

"After I kicked him off, you mean," Adam corrected.

Joe rolled his eyes. "Right. Well, what if he went and hired those guys to cut down some of your trees, just to stir up trouble?"

"Sure," Frank agreed. "And everybody must have heard on television that those so-called experts wanted to cut down your maples. That would have been a good cover for what they were doing."

"Now, hold on," Karl said, turning to Adam. "What was Nick doing at your place?"

Adam growled, "Trying to buy it, the big dirt worm."

"Was he now?" Karl said, raising one eyebrow. "He was by my place yesterday for the same reason. Said that with this poisoning scandal, I'd better sell now, while my land was still worth something."

"Wow!" Joe said to Frank. "You hear that?"

Adam turned to the Hardys and the girls. "Didn't I tell you?" he demanded. "Nick Unger wants to buy both our places and cut down the trees for some nutty strip mall. He must have sent over those dopes with the chain saws."

"We don't know that for sure," Frank said.

"We know he has some kind of sneaky plan up his sleeve," Karl said. "And I'm starting to wonder if he's behind the fire at my place, too." He narrowed his eyes. "Whatever he's up to, I'm not going to let him get away with it."

"Me either," Adam asserted. "I'd deed the place to a home for retired polecats before I'd let Onion Head have it."

"Well," Frank said. "It looks like you two finally agree on something."

Karl and Adam gave each other a surprised look.

"Huh," Adam muttered. "Just goes to show that even a no-brain old codger gets something right from time to time."

"Just what I was thinking," Karl growled. Then he caught Adam's eye and they both broke into laughter.

Karl went back home, his "wolf" at his heel. Callie, Vanessa, and Adam started back to the farmhouse, while Frank and Joe followed more slowly and talked over the case.

"Unger's looking more and more like our prime suspect," Frank declared. "We know he's taking advantage of the poisoning scare. The question is, did he create it, too?"

"He'd probably need an information source on the inside," Joe pointed out. "I still think Bob is a candidate. Why does he sneak around so much, if he's not up to something?"

Frank put his hand on Joe's arm, then silently pointed toward Adam's sugarhouse. Bob had just appeared around the corner of the shack with what looked like a thick chain in one hand and an ax handle in the other. He glanced toward the house, then slipped into the woods.

"Come on," Joe said.

They followed quickly. They soon lost sight of Bob, but his footprints in the snow were easy to track. Moving with care, they climbed the hill, using the thick tree trunks as concealment. They were nearing the crest when Frank heard a metallic clanking sound off to the right.

Frank held up a hand, then pointed. Joe gave a sharp nod. They moved off the trail into the underbrush, stepping high to clear the deeper patches of snow. Frank peered through the interlaced bare branches and held up his hand once more.

Bob was a dozen feet away, kneeling at the base of a tree with his back to the Hardys. Whatever he was doing was taking up all his attention. He pulled something apart with his hands. Then he placed something at the base of the tree, backed away, and began shoveling snow over it with his gloved hands.

Frank caught Joe's eye again. What was Bob doing—sabotaging the tree?

The hired hand clambered to his feet, using the ax handle to help push himself up, and started to turn. Then he froze, his head to one side as if listening to distant music.

Frank realized that this was someone who had lived all his life with the woods. He obviously sensed that he was being watched.

Before Bob could react, Frank gestured for Joe to move in on him from the left, while Frank took the right flank. "Go!" he whispered.

The Hardys rushed forward.

Bob straightened up and looked from one Hardy brother to the other. When he realized who they were, his shock turned to fury. He let out a fierce growl and raised the ax handle over his head, ready to swing. Frank dodged farther to the right, in a circling maneuver, while Joe ran straight toward the tree and whatever Bob had hidden there.

For one instant, Bob swung his gaze back and forth, confused. Then he turned away from Frank and rushed Joe. The ax handle whistled through the air, straight at Joe's head.

Chapter

9

"JOE! LOOK OUT!" Frank yelled.

Joe crouched down and covered his head with his arms.

The hardwood shaft of the ax skirted Joe and slammed into the ground at the base of the tree. Instantly something jerked up through the snow and closed around the ax with a loud metallic clang.

Joe stared down at the vicious teeth of a steel trap, only inches from his foot. Then he and Frank grabbed Bob by the arms and shoved him against the tree.

"What do you think you're doing?" Joe shouted into his face. He yanked Bob's jacket tight at the throat.

"You could've killed him," Frank added hotly.

Bob leaned back against the tree, making no effort to escape.

Joe shook him. "What're you doing here?" he demanded.

"Nothing. I wasn't doing anything. What're *you* doing here?" Bob demanded in return.

"You were doing something to these trees." Frank lowered his voice. "Maybe poisoning them."

"Not me," Bob said, a look of fear coming into his eyes. "I wouldn't do that."

Joe said, "You nearly killed me with that ax handle."

Bob shook his head. "You got me all wrong," he said. "I wasn't swinging at you. I was springing that bear trap. I was afraid you'd step on it and get hurt bad."

Joe looked down at the trap and took a deep breath. Then he released his grip on Bob's jacket and stepped back.

"A bear trap?" Frank echoed skeptically. "What are you doing with a bear trap?"

"That's an old trap of Adam's that I cleaned up and oiled," Bob replied. "I just wanted to see how it worked, that's all. I thought maybe we could use it to guard the sugar bush. But then when you came running out, I saw that it might hurt innocent people. So I sprang it."

Frank remembered the note that had been tied to the brick. Was it still in his pocket? He found it and held it under Bob's nose. "How about this?" he demanded. "Did you throw this through our window last night?"

Bob barely glanced at it. "What's it say?"

"You know what it says!" Joe said angrily.

Bob looked at the note, glanced up at Frank and Joe, then studied the note again.

Joe noticed something. Bob was holding the note upside down. "Bob?" he said. "Do you know how to read?"

Bob stared at the ground. In a low voice, he said, "Nope. But I mean to learn. Adam promised to teach me. But he gets real frustrated when I don't catch on right away."

Frank took back the note and met Joe's eyes. If Bob couldn't read, he couldn't write, either. And that meant he couldn't have typed the note. He still could have heaved it through their window, but that was looking more and more unlikely.

"You didn't have to scare me like that," Bob added.

"Sorry," Joe said.

"Adam's teaching me about sugaring, too," he continued. "I'm saving up. And one of these days, I'm going to have my own maple syrup business."

The Hardys walked with Bob back toward the farmhouse. "So what was in the red can you put in the trash barrel by the shed the other day?" Frank asked.

Bob stopped for a minute, a blank look on his face.

"When the cops were here," Joe prodded.

"Boy, you guys don't miss a trick," Bob said at last. Then he sighed and shook his head. "I was cleaning out the paint shelf in the barn, okay?"

"And then you emptied the trash can?" Frank pressed.

"Yup. Is that a crime or something?"

Frank let it drop. Clearly Bob was determined to hold on to his story.

Just before they reached the clearing, Bob stopped. "I've got to go this way," he said, taking a path that circled around to the left. Frank suspected why. Bob didn't want Adam to see him carrying the bear trap when he was supposed to be working.

At the farmhouse Frank and Joe found Adam piling split logs onto a canvas sling holder to carry inside for the cast-iron stove. They told him that they were now sure that Bob wasn't involved, and why.

"I'm not going to say I told you so," Adam said.

As they entered the kitchen, Callie called out, "We just had an idea. Vanessa and I were trying to figure out how to get the inside scoop on Unger."

"And I said we should find somebody with a grudge against him," Vanessa said. "People with grudges will tell you stuff that friends won't."

"Good idea," Frank said. "But how do we find someone like that?"

"There's a woman in town named Dottie Durkin," Callie told him. "I don't know how she feels about Unger, but I do know she knows everything about everybody's business. And she and Uncle Adam have been friends since grade school."

Joe said, "Great! Let's go."

"Why don't we kill two birds with one stone?" Frank suggested. "While you two see what you can find out from her, I'll swing by the town offices and see if I can dig up anything there about Nick Unger."

Before dropping off Frank at the town hall, the others agreed to meet him in an hour at the Soup Bowl Café, just down the street. Then they drove four blocks to Dottie Durkin's house. They rang the bell. A short, grandmotherly woman opened the door. When she saw Callie, she gasped, smiled, and put both hands across her heart.

"Adam phoned and said you were coming up," she exclaimed. "It is such a treat to see you, dear. And how you've grown! These must be your friends. Do come in."

Joe, Vanessa, and Callie followed Dottie into a living room full of knickknacks. After Callie introduced her friends, Dottie asked, "How is your uncle holding up? He sounded fine on the phone, but you know Adam. There's no telling what's going on inside that head of his."

"He's doing his best," Callie replied. "But it isn't easy for him. He's so proud of his syrup. To have everyone going around saying it's poison . . ."

"It must be terrible for him," Dottie said, giving a sympathetic cluck of her tongue. "The authorities had best find out what or who's really to blame, and do it soon, before poor Adam's life is wrecked."

"Oh, by the way," Joe said. "We just met somebody you probably know—Nick Unger."

Dottie scowled. "Oh? Where was this? Out at Shaw Farm, I wager. I hope Adam showed him the rough side of his tongue, too."

Vanessa laughed. "That's just about right, Ms. Durkin," she said.

"Oh, call me Dottie," the woman replied with a warm smile. "It was a sad day for Waterboro when Nick Unger moved here, I can tell you. Always sweet-talking folks into selling their farms to outlanders. They'd regret it later, of course, but not Old Nick. He'd just pocket his commission and go off looking for someone else he could hoodwink."

"Do you know what his current plans are?" Joe asked.

Dottie shook her head. "I'm much too busy with my needlepoint and my work at the town Historical Society to pay much mind to local gossip. But I can tell you who would know. Greg Toussaint, that's who. He was a partner in the real estate agency until he was forced out. I never heard the whole story, but it's my understanding that there is considerable bitterness between the two of them."

"Dottie?" Callie began tentatively. "Do you think Nick Unger would be capable of deliberately poisoning my uncle's maples?"

The older woman turned and walked to the mantel, where she rearranged a vase of dried flowers. With her back to the visitors, she said, "I don't hold with speaking ill of my neighbors. But I'll say this much. There isn't a lot I'd put past Nick Unger, if it meant a big real estate deal for him."

The three of them stayed a few minutes longer, admiring Dottie's needlepoint and looking at the photos on the mantel. Then they got directions to the home of Greg Toussaint.

Frank entered the Waterboro town office, where a wooden counter divided the room. A thin gray-haired woman with wire-rimmed glasses looked up from her work. "Can I do anything for you?"

Frank smiled. "I'm up at the university," he said, "and I'm doing a paper on current land use in the area. I'm hoping to interview people who have new developments in the works. Can you tell me if anybody's made any recent inquiries about zoning laws or building regulations around here?"

"Sorry, no," she said, and turned back to the file on her desk.

"Somebody mentioned a local developer named Unger," Frank persisted. "Do you happen to know if he's got any new projects on the drawing board?"

This time she didn't even look up. "Nope. Sorry."

"Well, thanks anyway," Frank said.

He was turning to go when she piped up. "Actually, I did have somebody in here the other day, but he was after something different."

"Oh? What was that?" Frank asked.

"He wanted to know if I thought the selectmen would agree to pay a percentage of the cost of installing new sewer and water lines and laying new roads in a big new development," the clerk told him. "He claimed the added property taxes would pay the town back in just a few years."

Frank stared at her. Someone had been asking about a big new development? This was exactly the kind of information he'd been hoping to get. "Who was he?" he asked eagerly. "Did he say where this development would be?"

The woman shrugged. "I never saw this man before. And he wasn't telling any more than he needed to."

"Thanks," Frank said. "You've been a big help."

"I don't quite see how," the woman said with a hint of a smile. "But you're welcome anyway."

Over burgers and fries at the Soup Bowl Café, the four friends exchanged findings and theories.

"The person who was asking those questions at the town office could have been working for Unger," Frank concluded.

"Sure," Vanessa said. "He wouldn't want to tip people off by asking himself."

"I say we go talk to this guy, Toussaint," Callie suggested.

"Great idea," Joe replied. "*After* I have a piece of that homemade lemon meringue pie!"

As they returned to the Hardys' van, Callie said, "Maybe just two of us should question this guy. Four seems like a bit much. Joe, why don't you drop me and Vanessa off at the farm first?"

The guys agreed, and once they let the girls out at Adam's place, they went in search of Unger's former partner. It turned out that he lived in a recently built house on the outskirts of town. A late-model luxury sedan was parked in the driveway.

They rang the bell, and Toussaint appeared in about a minute. He didn't want to ask them in, until Frank explained that they were working on an exposé of shady real estate practices and wanted to ask him about Nick Unger. Then his whole manner changed. "I've got plenty to say on that topic," he said with a sour expression. "Come on in."

He led them inside to a room furnished as an office. Toussaint was about forty, with a serious air about him. Frank had the feeling he didn't smile much.

"You used to be Unger's partner, didn't you?" Frank began. "We've heard that he has a big project in the works, and we're wondering if there's any connection between that and this poisoning scare out at Shaw Farm."

Toussaint stared at him, then at Joe. "Where on earth did you get that from?" he demanded.

"We're not at liberty to say," Joe replied. "But it was a reliable source. Can you tell us anything about this?"

The man hesitated, glancing back and forth between Frank and Joe. Finally he said, "Well, I can tell you this much—"

The phone rang. Toussaint picked it up and said, "Hello? Hello?"

His hand tightened on the receiver and his face turned pale. Slowly he put the receiver down and stared at it for a moment. Then he looked up at the Hardys with hardened eyes.

"Get out of my house, right now," he said. His voice rose almost to a shriek. "I mean it. Or I'll throw you out."

Chapter

10

"WHAT'S GOING ON?" Joe demanded. "Who was that call from?"

Toussaint raced to the window. After peering out, he lowered the shade. "Just get out—now!" he cried. "I can't talk to you."

Frank looked at him. "Was that Unger who called? Did he threaten you?"

"It wasn't anybody," the former real estate agent replied, wiping his forehead. "Will you leave, or do I have to call the police?"

"I don't think you really want to do that," Joe said. "Come on, tell us about the call. What got you so frightened?"

"I'm not frightened, I'm a busy man," he snapped.

"If you help us, Unger won't be in any shape

to bother you," Frank said as persuasively as he could. "That *was* him, wasn't it?"

"It was nobody," Toussaint repeated. "The line was dead. But, yes—that must have been Nick's way of warning me to keep my mouth shut. He must have followed you here. He knows you're onto him. And he thinks I'm going to squeal on him."

"How do you know it was him, if the line was dead?" Frank asked.

"He's done that before, when he thought I was going to the authorities about one of his schemes," Toussaint said. "He even admitted it."

"Until somebody exposes his activities, you'll never be safe from him," Frank pointed out. "But right now, if he knows we're onto him, he'll come after us, not you. What is he planning? Do you know?"

Toussaint sat in a chair. For a long time he just sat there, thinking. Finally he looked from Frank to Joe. "I saw a plan in his office one time. It took me a while to figure out where it was supposed to go, but I finally caught on."

"What was it?" Joe probed.

"A big condominium resort," Toussaint replied. "Bigger than anything around here, smack in the middle of Adam Shaw and Karl French's land."

Frank and Joe exchanged glances.

"But those old coots would never agree to sell their farms," Toussaint went on.

"So Unger had to do something that would make Adam and Karl want to sell their places," Frank jumped in. "Such as poisoning their syrup."

Joe frowned. "I thought the people around here didn't want any big condo resorts. How does Unger plan to get past that?"

Toussaint laughed bitterly. "You don't know how Nick works," he said. "All he needs to do is buy one or two selectmen. And he's probably bought them already."

"But meanwhile," Frank said, "he'll have to do his best to keep his plans secret."

Toussaint glanced at Frank. "Judging by what you fellows already know, it doesn't look like his best is going to be good enough, does it?"

Frank and Joe climbed back into the van.

"Based on what Toussaint said," Frank began, "Unger has a strong motive to poison Adam's syrup and to try to cut down his trees as scare tactics."

"That makes sense," Joe agreed. "But we still have at least one very big question to answer. How was the syrup poisoned?"

Frank nodded. "I wonder if the Health Department has found out anything definite," he said. "Didn't that Maas guy say he was from Concord?"

"Yeah—that's the state capital. Probably where the state health lab is, too," Joe said.

"Concord's just twenty miles away. What do you say we drop by?"

Joe started the engine. "You're on."

Once they reached Concord, the Hardys had little trouble locating Maas's office. He immediately recognized the brothers from the day before.

"What brings you two here?" Maas asked.

"We were wondering if your lab has found out anything new," Frank told him.

"That's really not public information," Maas replied. "But Chief O'Brien asked around about you two. It seems you have some pretty impressive references. The fact is, we still haven't found any poisons either in the remaining stock of syrup or in the stomach samples from the victims. However— and this is pretty puzzling—we did find that the syrup had an abnormal molecular structure."

"A mutation of some kind?" Frank suggested.

Maas nodded. "That's exactly what we're wondering. If so, it means—"

The office door flew open. A portly man with thinning gray hair, wearing a rumpled business suit, barged in.

"Gerald, I need to talk to you," he said, ignoring the Hardys. "I'm speaking for all the good people of Waterboro when I say that you have to straighten out this poisoned syrup thing, and fast."

Keeping his voice level, Maas introduced Frank and Joe to Hal Sloane, the head selectman of Waterboro. "Now, Hal," Maas continued, "take a deep breath and count to ten. As I told you yesterday, we're working on it."

"That's not good enough," Sloane replied. "If we don't get some action out of this office, every sugarer in the state is going to go belly-up. You've got the power to solve this. Do it. Issue a statement that this is an isolated case at Adam Shaw's farm, then put out an order to cut down Adam's sugar bush. Better be safe and cut down Karl French's, too. Whatever it is might have spread."

"That's a pretty drastic response," Maas said.

"It's a drastic situation." Sloane frowned. "And if you don't deal with it fast, it's just possible that some of the people it's ruining might decide to take matters into their own hands. Don't say I didn't warn you."

Before Maas could respond, Sloane spun on his heel and stalked out.

Maas shuffled some papers on his desk, clearly upset by his conversation with Hal Sloane. A moment later he looked back at the Hardys. "You'd better check back with me some other time, if you don't mind."

Frank knew that this wasn't the time to press Maas for more information. "Thanks for talking with us," he said. "Come on, Joe."

Back on the road, Frank said, "I have a strong

feeling that that guy Sloane is in Nick Unger's pocket."

Joe glanced at him. "You mean that Sloane's taking bribes from Nick Unger? Just as Toussaint warned us?"

Frank nodded. "Telling Maas to cut down all those trees just doesn't make sense otherwise. It's too early to suggest something that radical."

As Frank turned in to the drive at Shaw Farm, Vanessa and Callie came out on the porch, smiling.

"You'll never believe this," Callie called, when the two boys got out of the van. "Uncle Adam and Karl are working—"

"Together!" Vanessa cut in. "Isn't that incredible?"

"Yes," Joe said with a grin.

"Go see for yourselves," Vanessa suggested. "They're over at Karl's sugarhouse."

Frank and Joe followed the road across Adam's land and onto Karl's. At the burnt-out sugarhouse, they found the two neighbors working side by side, clearing away the debris.

The Hardys filled them in on what they'd learned at Maas's office.

Karl's face darkened. "No politician's going to be interfering in my business," he growled.

Adam gritted his teeth but didn't say anything for a minute. Then he gestured at the Hardys.

"Don't just stand there gawking. Get busy; help us clear up this mess."

Karl grabbed a shovel with one hand, a push broom with the other, and thrust them at Frank and Joe.

"There's work to do here," Adam grumbled. "This isn't a vacation, you know."

Frank was tempted to point out that it *was* a vacation for him, Joe, Callie, and Vanessa. In fact, it was supposed to be a cross-country skiing vacation! But the last thing he wanted to do just then was start an argument. He began sweeping the ashes and bits of charred wood toward the doorway, while Joe shoveled up larger pieces of debris.

"We're just back from the state Health Department in Concord," he remarked.

"Oh?" Adam said. "Karl here just had a visit from one of their staff. Wanted to sample his syrup production. Huh! Got nothing better to do, I suppose."

"He scraped some samples from what's left of my evaporator, too," Karl added. "Why, I don't know. He said it was for testing."

"You know what his test will show?" Adam asked. "That your sugarhouse burned down."

Karl laughed. "That's about right, too. So Adam and me, we decided to get a head start on clearing up the wreckage, before some turkey in Concord decides it's a public hazard."

"They would, too, the airheads," Adam snorted.

Frank was wrestling with a blackened, twisted remnant of the evaporator when he caught sight of someone just inside the woods. He was short and stocky, and wore a yellow and black ski mask over his face. He moved swiftly from tree to tree, apparently on snowshoes.

"Joe, look!" Frank whispered.

"He's doing something to the sap-collecting lines," Joe said.

Adam heard them talking. He turned to look. "Now, who would that be, and what's he up to?" he demanded angrily.

"Is Bob around?" Frank asked.

"Nope. That's not Bob," Adam answered. "He headed north for a few days to see his brother since the squash-head police closed down my sugarhouse."

"Come on, Frank," Joe said. "Let's find out what's up."

The Hardys dropped their tools and ran up the hill toward the woods. But the moment they left the trail, their feet sank six inches into the snow. It was like running through a lake of glue.

The man spotted them and immediately headed off over the top of the hill. On snow-shoes, he moved much faster than Frank and Joe. But they kept going, struggling through the thick snow. They forced themselves to the crest just in time to see their quarry tumble to the ground at the foot of the slope on the hill's other side.

"Hey, you!" Joe shouted. "Stop right there!"

The man struggled to his feet and tramped onward, leaving a trail of huge prints in the snow.

Panting, the Hardys kept after him, up another slope. By the time they reached the top, he was out of sight, but the trail of his snowshoes was easy to follow. It curved to the left, across a steep slope that ended at the edge of a cliff. The surface of the snow glistened where the clear sunlight was melting it.

Frank said, "We'd better try to catch him before he gets to the road."

He hurried forward, stomping to break through the thin crust of snow. Suddenly his right foot flew out from under him. The cycle of thawing and freezing had produced a thick layer of ice that was hidden by a dusting of snow. The hillside was as slippery as an Olympic bobsled run.

"Ow!" Frank shouted as he landed heavily on his side. Before he could even think about getting up, he started sliding down the slope, faster and faster. Frantic, he managed to roll onto his stomach and reach out to claw at the snow with both hands. But his desperate fingers found nothing to grip.

Finally he grasped a small, sharp outcropping of rock. His feet dangled in space.

"Hold on, Frank!" Joe yelled from above.

Frank twisted his head and looked below him. The cliff was sheer and at least forty feet high, with jagged boulders at the bottom. A fall like that would surely kill him.

Then he saw the man in the ski mask, down among the boulders. He caught Frank's eye and gave a jaunty wave goodbye.

Chapter

11

"HANG ON, FRANK! I'm coming," Joe shouted.

"No!" Frank screamed back. "It's too slick!"

Joe made a lightning-fast assessment of the situation. Frank's legs were dangling over the edge of the cliff. His face was gray from the strain of holding on to the rock outcropping. He couldn't possibly hang on for much longer.

Joe rapidly scanned the area. Just inside the woods, he noticed that a big branch from a white birch had broken off from the weight of the snow. It was three inches thick and at least twenty feet long—perfect for his needs. But could he manage to move it?

Joe grasped it and tried to lift. Nothing happened. The dead branch was as heavy as a stack of logs. Joe bent down, got a firmer grip, and put his back into it. This time the branch moved. He dragged it onto the slope.

"Hurry, Joe!" Frank called.

The dead wood slid easily down the hillside— *too* easily. Joe felt it slipping from his grasp. In another moment, it was going to go plunging downward, straight at Frank! Joe sat down on the snow and kicked his bootheels into the underlayer of ice, while gripping the branch tighter. After four tries, he managed to gain a strong foothold.

"Frank!" he called. "I'm going to slide this branch down next to you. Can you grab it?"

Frank's breath came out in a white cloud. "I don't know," he shouted. "It's just a little too far away."

Joe could see that if Frank let loose with one hand to grab the branch, he would be left hanging on to that rock with only his left hand. It was too risky. Joe tried to inch the branch closer, but it wouldn't move. One of its smaller branches was caught in the snow.

Oh, no, Joe thought, trying not to panic. If I don't do something soon, Frank's going to slide all the way down that slope.

Joe took a deep breath and let it out slowly, accumulating the inner force that martial arts experts call *chi.* Then, with renewed energy, he dug in his heels, and gave the tree branch a power-ful twist.

"That's it!" Frank called. "I think I can reach it now."

Joe looked down the slope. Frank shot out one hand toward the branch. The instant he grasped it, he pulled up his knees and got one foot on the rock. Then both feet.

"Just hold on," Joe told him. "I'll pull you up."

It took what seemed like forever, but slowly Joe managed to pull his brother up the slippery incline. At last the two brothers were standing together at the top of the ridge.

What a relief, thought Joe. For a few minutes he had thought it was all over for Frank.

"Thanks, Joe," Frank gasped. He leaned against the trunk of a nearby tree to catch his breath. "I needed that."

"You'll do the same for me someday." Joe grinned. "But for the meantime, let's just say you owe me another slice of that lemon meringue pie."

In response, Frank picked up a handful of snow and tossed it on Joe's head. Joe returned the favor.

"Come on," Frank said a moment later. "Let's head back. There's no point in trying to chase that dude. He's long gone."

They trudged back through the woods, follow-ing their own boot prints. As Karl's sugarhouse came in sight, Frank said, "That's the tree that guy was monkeying around with. You can tell by the snowshoe marks. I wonder what he was doing."

Joe went over to the tree and walked around it, carefully stepping only in the tracks left behind. There was a hollow at the base of the tree where the snow had melted. Joe was three quarters of the way around the trunk when a glint of gold caught his eye.

"Frank? I think I've found something," he called, without going closer. He pointed to the base of the tree. "Look."

Frank moved in and knelt down. "It's a wristwatch," he announced. He turned his head to one side and bent closer, without touching the watch. "There's an inscription on the back. *Tempus fugit*. 'Time flies.' And the engraved initials *N.U.* How about that?"

"Nick Unger!" Joe exclaimed. "I *thought* that man on snowshoes looked like him."

"We'd better leave everything just the way it is and get in touch with the police," Frank said.

"What if he comes back for his watch?" Joe asked.

Frank frowned. "We'll just have to risk that," he replied. "You know how often Dad has told us not to disturb important evidence."

Joe nodded. Their father, Fenton Hardy, was a famous detective who'd solved a lot of cases.

Joe knew he'd tell the boys to leave the scene undisturbed.

Adam and Karl saw them coming. "Gave you the slip, did he?" Karl asked wryly.

Frank and Joe looked at each other, remembering Frank's near miss with disaster. "You could put it that way," Frank told Karl.

"Well, for what it's worth, I called Chief O'Brien and told him about our trespasser," Karl said. "He should be along presently."

"While we're waiting, may I use your phone?" Frank asked. "And the phone book?"

Karl waved him toward the house. "Help yourself."

There were several jewelers listed in Concord, the largest nearby town. The first one didn't recognize Frank's description of the watch, and neither did the second.

The third one said, "Why, yes, I recall that. The Association of Real Estate Agents ordered a watch like that a couple of months ago to present to one of their members. A fellow named Unger, as I recall."

Frank replaced the receiver, looked up at Joe, and gave him a thumbs-up sign.

A car came up the lane and stopped in front of the house. Through the window, Frank saw Chief O'Brien and one of his officers get out and walk around to the back. By the time Frank and Joe got outside, Karl and Adam were already telling the chief about the intruder whom the Hardys had chased off.

Before the police officers could react, a line of cars and vans screeched to a stop behind the police cruiser. One of the vans had a satellite dish mounted on the roof.

Not *again*, Joe thought, as reporters, photographers, and camera crews spilled out of the cars and came rushing over to where O'Brien was standing with Adam and Karl. A battery of powerful television lights came on, aimed at the two sugarers.

"Chief?" someone called out. "Is it true that the maple plague has spread to this farm, too? One of the selectmen in town seems to think that there are plans to quarantine the infested area and cut down the diseased trees."

"No comment," O'Brien said.

Adam and Karl looked at each other. Adam raised one bushy white eyebrow, and Karl nodded. Then they pushed their way through the crowd to the toolshed built onto the side of the house. When they reappeared, Karl was carrying a metal tank with a hand pump built into the top. Adam held the sprayer wand that went with it. They stopped a few feet from the crowd of journalists. While Adam attached the hose to the wand, Karl pumped up the pressure.

"Now then," Karl said. "This here's my land, and I don't recollect inviting any of you onto it.

How would it be if you packed up and left, right now?"

"Mr. French," one of the reporters said, holding out his microphone. "Is it true that the sap from your maple trees is poisonous, just like the sap from Shaw Farm?"

The crowd moved closer to catch Karl's answer.

He smiled grimly. "I'll give you a chance to find that out for yourselves," he said. "Adam?"

Adam raised the sprayer wand and pressed the trigger. A thin stream of liquid shot out and hit the ground just in front of the newshounds. They all took a step backward.

"Last time I only dipped one of your cameras," Adam reminded them. "Karl here believes in the wholesale approach. Either you get off his property, or you get sprayed. Which is it to be?"

He pressed the trigger again. This time the line of liquid hit the feet of the crowd.

Frank looked over at Joe with a grin.

The news crowd was silent. They stared at the two crusty men, then at the nozzle in Adam's hand.

"Which is it?" Adam repeated. He jerked the spray closer and closer to the crowd.

Connie Page was in the crowd, with a look of outrage on her face. She turned on O'Brien. "Are you going to let them get away with this?" she demanded.

The police chief shrugged. "It's his land," he said. "I came here on another matter, but if he asks me, I just might have to arrest you for trespassing."

Good for him, Frank said to himself.

Karl bent down to pump up the pressure again, and Adam jerked the hose closer.

"All right," a cameraman said. "We're going. Just don't spray that stuff on my equipment. Or me," he added.

As the crowd hurried away, Karl picked up the tank by its strap. He and Adam followed the mob to their cars, encouraging them with more squirts from the sprayer.

As the cars started to back away, Adam said, loud enough for everyone to hear, "Imagine—grown-ups afraid of a little well water!"

Then he and Karl started to cackle. Karl bent over and slapped his thigh with glee. Frank caught Joe's eye, and they began to laugh, too.

O'Brien looked at them with a straight face, but Frank was sure there was a twinkle in his eye. Finally he said, "All right, fun's over. What's all this Karl was telling me?"

Joe and Frank told him about spotting and chasing the intruder, then finding the wristwatch. "I confirmed that it belongs to Unger," Frank concluded. "You can check that with Vail's Jewelers in Concord."

"Where's this watch?" O'Brien demanded.

"We left it where we saw it. We didn't want to disturb the evidence."

O'Brien gave a nod of approval. "The folks I spoke to were right—you *are* good detectives. What did this fellow look like?"

Frank and Joe took turns describing him, reporting that the man was about five foot six, a hundred fifty pounds, wearing a heavy down parka and a full-face yellow-and-black ski mask with a red tassel on top. "He moved fast," Joe added, "but sort of jerkily, as if he wasn't too used to snowshoes."

"A down parka?" O'Brien asked. "That would keep you from getting a real idea of his build. And you didn't see his face at all, right? So you don't really know that it was Nick."

Karl stepped up. "I saw him, and so did Adam. What I say is, if it looks like a Nick, walks like a Nick, and acts like a Nick, it's a Nick."

Joe laughed. Then he froze. "Frank!" he whispered. "There he is! He's back!"

He pointed up the hill. Then, without another word, he and Frank sprinted toward the intruder. The man saw them coming, hesitated, then turned and ran. This time he wasn't wearing his mask. It was clearly Nick Unger.

Joe was a few feet in the lead when the two brothers reached the crest of the slope. Unger was barely fifty feet away, struggling through the thick snow. He gave a panic-stricken look over his shoulder and ran straight into a tree. By the time he recovered, Joe and Frank had almost caught up to him. He struggled to his feet, ran another ten feet, and fell to his knees next to a big maple. Half-buried in the snow, he turned around like a trapped animal. Terror flared in his eyes as Frank and Joe closed in on him. Groping in the pocket of his parka, he pulled out a small but deadly automatic and aimed it with a shaking hand right at Joe's head.

Chapter

12

FRANK AND JOE FROZE just a few feet away from the terrified real estate agent.

"Stay back," Unger warned. The pistol wavered between Joe and Frank. "I mean it; I'll shoot!"

Frank spoke calmly, as if he were talking to a spooked horse. "Take it easy, Mr. Unger," he said. "Nobody has to get hurt. We can work this out."

"Don't move!" Unger said, his voice quavering.

"Don't worry, we're not moving," Joe told him. He held his arms out from his sides, the open palms showing.

"We don't want you around here," Unger continued. "A couple of outsiders, trying to ruin everything. Why don't you leave me alone?"

Frank sensed that the man's panic was increasing. With every second, the situation was becoming more perilous. What would Unger do if O'Brien and the other police officer appeared unexpectedly? One twitch of his finger, and at best, either Frank or Joe would be badly wounded. At worst . . . Frank decided he didn't even want to think about it.

"Mr. Unger, you saw Chief O'Brien down there with us, didn't you?" he asked in a soothing voice. "He'll be here any minute. You don't want him to see you like this, do you?"

"I can handle him *and* you two," Unger replied, his hand shaking. "You deserve it, for trying to frame me this way."

Joe stared at him for a second. Frame him? Is that what Unger really believed?

"We aren't trying to frame you," Joe replied. "You're the one who tried to lure us off that cliff, after we spotted you poisoning Karl's maples."

"Did you get your watch?" Frank asked. "Or is it still there, for Chief O'Brien to find?"

Unger gripped the automatic in both hands and aimed it at Frank. "I knew it!" he declared. "Which one of you stole it from me?"

"We found it where you dropped it," Joe told him. "While you were poisoning the trees."

Unger didn't seem to hear. "You probably

think you're pretty clever, getting me up here with that fake phone call," he said. "You didn't think I'd bring a gun, did you?"

"What phone call?" Frank asked.

"Don't pull that," Unger said. "You called me and told me my watch was near a specific tree on French's farm, and that the cops would think it was proof that I was behind the syrup poisoning."

Frank studied the frightened man's face. Could he possibly be telling the truth? he wondered.

Unger's gaze shifted past Frank and Joe, and Frank knew that the two police officers were approaching. He glanced over his shoulder and saw them draw their revolvers.

"Nick Unger!" O'Brien called, his voice sounding hollow over the cold distance. "Is that you, Nick?"

"Stay back!" Unger shouted. "Or these two get it!"

Joe thought fast. "Mr. Unger," he said. "Now's the time to end this without anybody getting hurt. We won't press charges."

Nick looked at Joe, then up at the two officers.

O'Brien called, "Nick, we've known each other awhile. Let's stop this foolishness, before it's too late. I need you to answer some questions, that's all."

Nick shouted back, "I didn't do anything."

"I'm not saying you did," O'Brien told him.

"Nick, I'm putting away my weapon, and so is Will. Now it's up to you."

The cornered real estate agent hesitated, looking between the Hardys and the officers up the hill. Then he lowered the gun and stared at it, as if he wasn't quite sure what it was doing there.

Joe took a deep breath and let it out slowly.

Police Chief O'Brien and his officer walked down the snow-packed hill, took Unger's pistol from him, and helped him up the slope.

Back at Karl's farmhouse, the Hardys and the two old sugarers watched the police car drive away. Then Frank and Joe told them about the confrontation and recounted what Nick had said about the watch.

"That skunk hasn't told the truth about *anything* since the day he decided to go into real estate," Karl said. "Why believe him about this? Mysterious phone calls, my foot!"

"With luck, O'Brien will get the truth out of him," Frank said. "And even if he doesn't, I don't think you have to worry about Mr. Unger's building a resort in place of your sugar bush."

Karl gave Adam a slap on the back. "What do you say, neighbor?" he demanded. "Now that Nick is out of the way, why don't we give these city folks a treat they won't forget? One more sugaring session before the spring sets in for good."

"Finest kind," Adam rumbled. "But with your

sugarhouse blown up and mine tied up, we'll have to do it the old-fashioned way."

"All right with me," Karl said with a nod and a smile. "We can do it right here."

"Wow," Joe said. "That sounds great!"

"I'll call Callie and Vanessa," Frank said.

Karl pointed to his house. "Phone's right in there, as you probably remember."

"But what *is* the old-fashioned way?" Joe asked.

"You'll see," Karl said. His blue eyes twinkled.

As dusk fell, Callie and Vanessa arrived with a picnic basket stuffed with ham and cheese sandwiches and fresh fruit. The group quickly gobbled up the supper, then got ready for Karl and Adam's sugaring session.

Joe and Vanessa stacked split spruce and oak logs in Karl's backyard, while Frank and Callie shoveled away the snow and dug a shallow fire pit in the frozen ground. They all helped build a stack of logs, topped with some kindling. Callie took a kitchen match and lit it. As the flames grew, casting long shadows across the snow, they fed the fire with sweet-smelling spruce logs. Adam told them that the resin-rich softwood would burn fast to get the fire going. Then they added the denser hardwood oak logs that burned long and hot.

Meanwhile, Adam and Karl were busy sterilizing the filters, testers, sap pails, syrup jugs, and a huge black iron kettle. Then they set up a system of iron poles and bars, attached the wire bail of the kettle to a dangling hook on the crossbar, and turned the gears to lower the kettle over the bed of sizzling, red-hot oak coals.

"We'll use this leftover sap from last year," Karl said, "just in case."

"You old Yankee skinflint," Adam said, smiling. "Well, it's not poisoned, that's for sure."

Karl poured the sap from a five-gallon jug into the kettle. On the side of the huge kettle, he hung a small iron pot filled with corn oil.

With the fire burning bright red and the crisp, frosty night full of bright white stars overhead, it was a grand celebration.

From the kitchen Karl brought a mixing bowl of dough, paper plates, napkins, and a slotted spoon. "Hush puppies!" he said, and put the tray down on a nearby tree trunk.

"What're those?" Joe asked, looking curiously at the yellow mixture.

The maple sap was bubbling and steaming now, thickening into syrup and sending out a delicious aroma. "While we're waiting for the main event," Adam said, "we're going to fry up some tasty tidbits."

The Hardys, Callie, and Vanessa gathered around Karl and Adam as they scooped up marble-size portions of the cornmeal and onion mix, rolled them into balls, and tossed them into the small pot of boiling oil. When the dough fried up puffy and golden brown, Adam scooped them from the hot oil with a slotted spoon, put them on paper plates to cool, and said, "Dig in."

"Wow!" Joe was the first to sample a hush puppy. "These are great!"

Karl began rolling more and tossing them in the oil.

"Why are they called hush puppies?" Frank asked.

"Well, I'll tell you," Karl said, peering into the pot to check the progress of the second batch. "First off, they come from the South."

"South New Hampshire?" Adam asked, teasing.

"Close. They started when people like us were having a good time out in the woods cooking up this and that. Only the dogs knew it, too. Those dogs kept barking and yapping. They wanted whatever their masters were eating. So someone grabbed a handful of these goodies and threw them to the dogs. And as he did it, he called, 'Hush, puppies!' So that's what they're called."

"Arf, arf!" Joe said. "Let's have some more."

Frank handed one to Callie. "No, thanks. I'm saving room for the syrup," she explained.

"Besides," Frank teased, "fried foods are bad for your figure."

109

"With all those winter clothes on, how can you tell?" Joe demanded.

Vanessa poked him just below the ribs and said, "If I were you, I wouldn't talk about other people's figures."

"That's one hundred percent muscle," Joe protested.

"This bears watching," Adam said to them. He and Karl were taking turns lowering a cooking thermometer into the bubbling dark syrup. "Two twenty-one—the magic number," he said. "It's ready."

Everyone cheered.

"But first," Karl announced, "we're going to make some instant maple sugar candy."

"All right!" Joe said.

"How do you do that?" Frank asked.

"Watch." Karl filled a ladle with boiling hot syrup from the kettle, while Adam built up a mound of snow. Karl poured the syrup over the snow. There was a hiss and a puff of steam. When it cleared, Frank saw that the hot syrup had hardened into a creamy solid.

"Easy as pie," Karl said with a grin. "Callie, you're elected to take the first bite because you're the one who brought us together."

The others shouted in agreement.

Callie tasted it and smiled broadly. Then the group started on the fresh maple syrup, taking sip after sip until Joe came up with the idea of dunking hush puppies into it.

As the fire died down, Joe decided to lead everyone in a chorus of "One hundred jars of syrup on the wall . . ."

They had gotten all the way to ninety-two jars when Adam growled, "Hush, puppies! That's enough."

Everyone laughed.

After helping Karl and Adam clean up and put away the pots, the young sugarers thanked the older men for the treat.

"Callie," Karl said, "I'll pour the rest of the syrup into this jar, and you can take it back to Adam's place for tomorrow."

"Or tonight," she said, smiling.

"These peanut butter jars are good and wide at the top," Karl said as he tilted the kettle. "We use them all the time."

Karl waved as the others walked through the moonlit snowy woods to Adam's cozy farmhouse.

On the way Frank realized that they had all had such a great time that they'd forgotten about Adam's and Karl's troubles. For the moment.

In the kitchen Callie put her syrup jar next to the others on the counter, while her uncle busied himself stoking the cast-iron stove. Joe and Vanessa went outside and came back with enough split logs to refill the woodbox.

Frank glanced over at Callie and caught her

sneaking a long sip of maple syrup from one of the jars. Smiling, she screwed on the lid, then held a finger to her lips. Her uncle caught the movement and gave her a suspicious glance.

In the living room, Vanessa said, "Let's skip the news tonight. Are there any old movies on?"

Joe found the local paper and checked the listings. "Who's for Charlie Chan?" he asked.

Two hours later, when the movie ended, Callie was the first to stand up. As she did, she let out a moan and clutched her stomach with both hands.

Frank jumped to his feet and took her in his arms. "What is it?" he asked, looking in horror at her contorted face.

Callie let out another anguished cry, then gasped for breath. Her nails dug into Frank's arms. Suddenly she screamed and doubled over.

Chapter
13

FRANK HELD CALLIE TIGHTER. "What's wrong?" he asked. Over her shoulder, he met Vanessa's eye. He could see that Vanessa was thinking the same horrible thought as he was.

"My stomach," Callie moaned. "It hurts." She was trembling. Her face turned dead white, and she started to collapse to the floor.

"We've got to get her to a hospital fast," Frank said, supporting her weight.

Joe grabbed their winter jackets. "Let's go."

"I'll get a blanket," Vanessa said. Adam handed her one that he had just grabbed from the linen closet.

Frank carried a moaning, blanket-wrapped Callie to the van. Joe, at the wheel of the Hardys' van, sped through the snow-edged roads to Reed Regional Hospital. He steered the van through the parking lot to the emergency entrance.

Carrying Callie, Frank hurried through the door, with Joe and Vanessa right behind him. The nurse on duty jumped up and motioned for Frank to follow her into the emergency examining room.

The nurse pulled back the curtain. Frank laid Callie on the black leather table. She kept moaning while the nurse unwrapped the blanket.

"Okay, don't worry. We'll handle this," the nurse said.

The doctor on duty hurried in. "Would you wait outside, please?" he said to Frank, Joe, and Vanessa.

In the waiting room, they looked at each other with worry in their eyes. Long moments passed, then the nurse approached them. "Did she take any medications or eat anything unusual?"

"Maple syrup," Frank told her grimly.

The nurse tightened her lips. "I was afraid of that."

"But we all had the syrup," Vanessa interjected. "Callie's the only one of us who got sick."

Joe sat there, thinking. Why had Callie become ill when everyone else was fine? He looked at Frank. "Callie didn't have any of the hush puppies—did she?"

"Hush puppies?" The nurse looked puzzled.

"Sort of like deep-fried cornbread," Vanessa explained. "We all ate them, except for Callie."

"Right. Thanks." The nurse rushed back into the examining room.

"Good thinking, Joe." Frank turned to his brother. "Callie didn't have any of the hush puppies. But how could something that she *didn't* eat make her sick?"

For a moment his question hung in the air. No one knew the answer.

As the three of them waited to hear about Callie, they anxiously paced the floor of the waiting room.

Callie had obviously been in a lot of pain— Frank hoped she'd be okay.

Finally the doctor came out and told them he had pumped out Callie's stomach. "She's stabilized," he added with a faint smile. "I'm sure she'll be fine now, but I'd like to keep her here overnight, just in case."

"What caused this?" Frank asked. "Was it the syrup?"

The doctor shrugged. "All I can say at this point is that her symptoms are the same as the others who've eaten the syrup and become ill."

"But this time we all ate it," Joe said. "Why was Callie the only one affected?"

"It's conceivable that the oil you ate with the fried hush puppies coated the lining of your stomachs," the doctor explained. "That could have prevented whatever is in the syrup from giving you trouble." He paused. "Or Callie may simply be more susceptible than the rest of you."

Later, the Hardys and Vanessa visited Callie in her room.

"I can't believe so much pain could come from so much fun," she said, still pale and weak from her ordeal. "Something is really wrong. We've got to find out what's in that syrup."

"We will," Frank promised her. "For now we're just glad you're okay." He gave her a kiss and added, "We'll pick you up in the morning. Get some rest."

The next morning, Frank, Joe, and Vanessa got in the van to drive to the hospital. As they neared the turnoff to Karl's farm, Joe said, "What's going on here?"

A line of cars and vans was parked on the shoulder of the narrow lane. Joe slowed down, then stopped near a dense pack of reporters and camerapeople.

Frank peered over the heads of the crowd. "It's that guy we saw on TV the other night," he reported. "Remember? The one who said he'd invented some new kind of maple syrup. Gagnon, or something like that."

"They never stop, do they?" Vanessa said, looking with distaste at the newspeople.

"I know what must have happened," Frank

said. "Somebody assigned to watch the hospitals found out about Callie, and the word spread that the syrup came from Karl's farm."

Joe pulled ahead and parked, and the three friends piled out to stand at the back of the mob. Frank, at six one, could see over the newspeople's heads. Connie Page was standing next to Gagnon, microphone in hand.

"... the same symptoms as the other victims," Gagnon was saying. "But this time it came from the farm next door to Adam Shaw's, which belongs to Karl French. The conclusion is obvious. The public has to realize that eating this natural maple syrup is a high-risk proposition. And the danger is obviously spreading."

Connie Page lifted her hand mike closer to him. "Farmers in New England have been making maple syrup for hundreds of years," she pointed out. "Why is this happening now, in your opinion?"

Good question, thought Joe.

Gagnon looked straight into the camera. "This is a different world today," he said. "Acid rain, pesticides, toxic waste, nuclear fallout ... Who knows exactly what happened? Maybe all these toxins joined in a horrible combination to bring about this disaster."

Connie started to ask another question, but Gagnon continued. "As far as I'm concerned, it's too dangerous to take any chances. I'm going to stay away from uncontrolled products. And I'm going to do my best to get poisonous syrup off the market, and see that the trees that produced that syrup are cut down, before they infect others."

He turned and pointed up the hill, toward Karl's sugar bush. The cameras panned in that direction, then back to him.

"One more thing, Connie," Gagnon said. "The good people of our area should know that they don't have to give up their maple syrup because of this tragedy. Fortunately, they can now select a superior grade of man-made syrup—Gagnon's Gold."

"Is this a news broadcast?" Joe muttered. "Or a commercial?"

Frank made a face. "Come on, let's get out of here. Callie's waiting for us."

At the hospital, they found Callie looking like her old self, smiling and rosy-cheeked. "Am I glad to see you!" she said, giving Frank a big hug. "How's Uncle Adam doing?"

"He's pretty upset," Joe admitted. "But glad to hear that you're okay."

As they started out of the hospital, Frank said, "I wonder if the lab here found out anything about what happened to you, Callie."

"I thought the state lab in Concord was handling all this," Vanessa said.

Frank nodded. "It is, as far as I know. But the hospital lab must be in on it, too. Callie, can you stand hanging around this place for a few more minutes?"

"I'm fine," Callie replied. "Besides, we've got to get to the bottom of this. I don't want anybody else to go through what I went through."

They found the lab and knocked on the door. A tall, thin man with tortoiseshell glasses opened it. The name tag on his white lab coat read Eric Wright, NH Department of Health. Frank explained who they were and what they wanted.

"So you're our latest victim," the technician said to Callie. "You're the reason I came down from Concord. I'm glad to see you up and around. Come on in."

Inside, Joe asked Wright if his tests had uncovered the reason for Callie's illness.

"No, I'm sorry to say," he replied. "As far as we can tell, the syrup she ate was pure—no foreign substances, no pollutants, nothing."

"Then you're at a dead end?" Joe asked.

"Not quite," Eric said. "We're starting to approach this from another direction. Maple syrup is a basic, simple sugar. It's composed of six elements, including sodium, calcium, and iron. Normally they all pass right through the stomach and are filtered through the liver without any problem."

"The liver is supposed to filter out poisons from the blood, isn't it?" Frank asked.

"That's right," Eric replied. "The liver is the largest glandular organ in the human body and performs about five hundred different functions."

"Wow!" Joe said. "That many?"

The man nodded. "But the most important functions are regulation of the blood chemistry and detoxification, that is, filtering out harmful substances."

"So because Callie didn't eat those fried foods to coat her stomach," Frank said, "the poisons in the syrup were absorbed through the stomach and reached her liver."

Eric paused. "I can't say that positively without more evidence. I wouldn't have thought that the oil alone would have been enough to protect you three. And, as I said, we haven't yet managed to isolate any contaminant in the syrup. In fact, it's beginning to look as if we're dealing with an alteration in the makeup of the syrup itself."

"A mutation?" Joe asked.

Eric shook his head. "Not necessarily," he said. "But if the molecular structure of the syrup has somehow been changed, it might have created something that is too large to be properly filtered by the liver. In that case, it would accumulate and cause serious effects—severe pain, damage to the balance of the blood chemistry, even death if not caught in time. At this point, we're taking a very close look at some of the iron compounds in the samples."

Vanessa wrinkled her nose. "I thought iron was good for you."

"It is," Eric told her, "if taken in the right quantity. But megadoses, no. Any substance can be a poison if you take in too much. For example, Arctic natives never eat the liver of polar bears, which has a very high, toxic concentration of vitamin A. They'd die of a vitamin overdose."

"That's weird," Joe said.

"But true," Eric remarked.

The four friends thanked the technician for his help and returned to the van. As they drove out of town, Callie said, "You know, something just occurred to me."

Frank glanced at her, a quizzical look on his face.

"Remember when I took an extra sip of syrup after we got back to Adam's?" she went on. "Maybe my food poisoning didn't have anything to do with the hush puppies. Maybe *that* syrup was tainted."

"But wasn't that from the jar filled with the pure stuff we cooked up last night?" Frank asked.

Callie put her hand beneath her chin and frowned. "I thought so at the time. But there were several other jars on the counter—all from this year's harvest. What if I mixed up one of them with the syrup we made?"

"It's possible," Joe commented from the backseat. "Those peanut butter jars all look exactly alike."

Frank sighed. "That could explain why you got sick and we didn't. But no matter how you got poisoned, we're up against a very sophisticated plot. Whoever's involved obviously knows a lot about chemistry."

"Do you think that guy Unger has the scientific background to carry it out?" asked Callie.

"No," Frank replied.

"He could dig the information out of books," Joe suggested. "Or hire someone who does know how."

Vanessa shook her head. "I agree with Frank," she said. "Unger's the kind of creep who might set fire to Karl's sugarhouse to get him to sell out, but this chemical stuff just doesn't fit."

Frank turned onto the narrow lane to Shaw Farm. As he reached the drive, he slowed down, then stopped completely.

Three police cars were parked halfway up the drive, a few of their doors still open. In the distance, he could see a swarm of blue-uniformed officers around Adam's sugarhouse.

Then Chief O'Brien's voice rang out, amplified by a bullhorn. "Give up, you two—or I'll order my men to move in."

"What now?" Callie moaned.

"I don't know," Frank said. "But we'd better find out."

As Frank put the van in gear again, Adam's voice rang out through the woods.

"I'm not moving an inch—even if you shoot me dead in my tracks!"

Chapter

14

THE SECOND FRANK PULLED the van to a stop, the foursome piled out and raced to the sugarhouse. They pushed to the front of the crowd, where Chief O'Brien was standing, tense and grim-faced.

"We need your help," he said when he saw them.

Frank gaped at him. "With what?"

The chief gave him a tired look. "See for yourself."

As he stood aside, Frank saw Adam and Karl, sitting against the open door of the sugarhouse. A heavy chain crisscrossed their chests and ran through the gap at the hinge side of the door.

Oh, no, Frank thought. I don't believe these two.

The two men had chained themselves together, then locked themselves to the sugarhouse. Now their defiant faces were puckered up like old Halloween pumpkins.

"They're protesting the fact that Gerald Maas closed down Adam's sugaring operation—or so the two old fools claim," O'Brien said, rolling his eyes.

"Are they all right?" Callie asked.

O'Brien nodded. "Oh, sure. They're fine. Though I think they might be starting to get a bit chilly. Will you try to talk some sense into them?"

"Why don't you just go in there with some big cutters?" Joe asked.

O'Brien pressed his lips together. "We were about to do that. It'd take about seven seconds. But . . ."

"It wouldn't look so great on the six-o'clock news, would it?" Frank said, finishing the chief's thought for him. " 'Police manhandle old-timers.' "

"Let's find out what Karl and Adam have to say," Joe said. "It's their protest, after all."

The foursome walked up to the two sugarers.

"Uncle Adam?" Callie asked. "What on earth are you two up to?"

"Hello, Callie. Glad you're up and around," Adam replied. "You don't blame me for your sickness, do you? I'd hate to think you did."

124

"Or me?" Karl asked.

"Don't be ridiculous," Callie said emphatically.

"Good," Adam said. "Because I been thinking. That syrup we made by kettle last night was from Karl's sap from last year. And they're saying people got sick from this year's sap. So it couldn't have been from what we boiled up last night."

Callie nodded. "I thought of that myself," she said. "I must have taken a sip from one of the other jars on the counter."

"I set those aside so they could be tested by somebody impartial," Adam told her. "I guess I needn't bother. The stuff's obviously poison." He shook his head and looked away from Callie.

"Oh, Uncle Adam." Callie put her hand on his arm. "It's not your fault. We'll figure out what's going on." She pointed to the chains on Adam and Karl. "What are you two doing?"

"We're protesting police tyranny," Adam replied, giving Chief O'Brien a defiant look. "And we're going to stay here until that soot-faced boot Nick Unger is put away and we're allowed to get back to sugaring."

"Adam," O'Brien said, "we took Nick in for questioning, that's all. He's not under arrest."

"Then he should be," Karl growled. "That mealymouthed wheeler-dealer bombed my sugarhouse. Came mighty close to bombing *me,* too!"

"The minute I find solid evidence, I'll arrest him," O'Brien promised. He pointed to the yellow ribbon. "But meanwhile, you broke through an official barrier. That's an infraction."

"It was in our way," Adam said calmly.

"Please, Uncle Adam," Callie pleaded. "You've made your point. I don't want you to catch pneumonia, sitting out here."

Frank said, "This year's sugaring season is ninety percent done anyway, isn't it?"

Adam and Karl looked at each other. "Maybe so, maybe not," Adam said.

"I'll tell you what," Frank proposed. "If I try to set up those independent lab tests you want, will you unchain yourselves?"

Adam and Karl grumbled and snorted and shifted around. They looked again at each other. Then, to Frank's relief, Adam reached into his parka pocket and produced the key to the padlock.

Chief O'Brien tried to help the two old men to their feet, but they pushed him aside. Shaking his head in amusement, the police chief told his assistant that it was time for them to leave. As O'Brien climbed into the police car, he shouted to Adam and Karl, "But no more of these pro-tests, you hear? My health won't stand it!"

Over a lunch of scrambled eggs, homemade sausage, and toast, Frank and Joe talked over plans with Vanessa, Callie, Adam, and Karl.

"Where are we going to find an independent

lab that's equipped for the sort of analysis we need?" Frank wondered.

"I know," Vanessa said. "Remember that guy who was mouthing off to the newspeople this morning—Gagnon? He must have quite a lab setup if he was able to produce maple syrup through genetic engineering."

"Yeah, but he's not going to want to help us out," Joe said. "He's planning to get rich off this situation."

"What if you find someone who can give us access to his lab after hours?" Callie suggested.

"We'd also need somebody with the skills to run the tests," Frank pointed out. "Hmm— maybe that fellow we met at the hospital this morning. I think I'd better get busy on the phone."

Frank's first call was to his father. Fenton Hardy listened to the problem and promised to do what he could. It was a long shot, but Fenton had made a lot of contacts in his years as a detective; Frank was hoping he could hook them up with somebody who knew someone at the plant.

Twenty minutes later, Fenton called back with the name and number of a worker at Gagnon's plant, a man named Garrick.

"He's not too hot about doing this," Fenton warned. "He only agreed to let you in because he's a friend of an old college buddy of mine. He says it's tonight or not at all."

"Thanks, Dad," Frank said. He hung up, then called the hospital and asked to speak to Eric Wright.

Frank explained the situation to the technician. At first Eric flatly refused to help. Then Frank told him how desperate Karl and Adam were getting. "Their reputations are at stake—and so is the whole sugaring industry in this state," he concluded.

"All right," Eric finally said. They agreed to meet near Gagnon's plant that evening.

Frank hung up the phone with a triumphant expression. "Bingo," he told the others. "We have a lab and someone to help us analyze the syrup."

It was two hours after closing time at Gagnon's plant. Frank, Joe, and Eric went to the back entrance and knocked. The man who opened the door blinked nervously. "Three of you? I thought it was just two. I don't like surprises."

"We won't take long," Frank assured him.

Garrick hesitated but finally let them in and led them to the lab. "You'd better be quick," he said. "I'm outta here. You never saw me." He hurried off.

Eric stopped in the doorway and looked at the array of high-tech equipment. "This is amazing," he said. "Some of this is real cutting-edge, much more advanced than what we have at the state lab."

Eric headed straight to the gas chromatograph, which analyzed the chemical composition of compounds. He inserted samples of sap and syrup from Adam and Karl's maples, including some from the jars in Adam's kitchen. A couple of minutes later, he was scanning the printouts.

"No additives of any kind," he reported in a preoccupied voice. "The only thing that's unusual is a slight variation in ferrous compounds—in other words, iron."

While Eric continued to work at the gas chromatograph, Frank wandered around the lab. On a stone-topped table near the wall was a row of test tubes filled with clear and amber-colored liquids. They were labeled and dated as samples of maple sap, with varying degrees of sugar concentrations. Next to these were two more rows of low, circular petri dishes labeled "yeast."

"Eric?" Frank called. "Why would they be keeping maple sap and yeast on the same work table?"

Eric looked up, then came over and scanned the table. "Hmm," he said. "I think you just found something very, very interesting. I suspect that this lab is working on producing syrup by injecting engineered maple genes into yeast."

Joe joined them. "Yeast is alive, right?"

The technician nodded. "Yes," he replied.

"And it multiplies very fast. That's what makes bread rise. Apparently they've gotten these injected yeasts to yield a compound that's like that of maple sap. Once it's filtered out and concentrated, I don't know that you could even tell it apart from maple syrup from trees."

Frank frowned. "And it could be produced all year-round, too, whatever the weather. Hey, wait," he added, his eyes brightening. "If Gagnon can engineer maple genes this way, maybe he's also found a way to change the genes, not for the better—but for the worse. What would happen if he somehow put those altered genes into trees? Would it cause the trees to produce dangerous sap?"

Eric scratched his chin. "I guess it's possible, in theory," he said cautiously.

"Sure!" Joe said excitedly.

"It might have something to do with an enlarged ferrous compound molecule that I was just studying with the electron microscope." Now Eric sounded as excited as Frank or Joe. "I'd better double-check."

While Eric went on with his work, Frank and Joe continued to inspect the lab. Frank was looking at the array of test tubes again when Joe called to him. He was standing by the open door of a closet. When Frank joined him, he said, "Does that look familiar?"

On the floor of the closet was a backpack-style

sprayer. It looked just like the one Frank had seen on the back of the intruder at Karl's house.

"Maybe that guy at Karl's wasn't Unger," Frank said. "Unless Unger is working with Gagnon."

"It's possible, isn't it?" Joe said. "Unger has a strong motive, after all."

"So does Gagnon—given the fact that it couldn't hurt to knock out his pure maple syrup competition," Frank pointed out. "And frankly, with a lab like this, he seems like a better suspect than Unger. But what we need now is real, hard evidence."

Joe swiveled his head to survey the room. "Did you check out that freezer yet?" he asked. "I doubt they keep it here just to store their frozen fruit snacks."

Frank followed Joe across to the freezer.

Joe took the handle and tugged. Nothing happened. "Locked, maybe," he muttered, and tugged harder.

The freezer door swung open. Instantly a piercing alarm began to sound in the hall outside. Frank had just enough time to glimpse a canister labeled Biohazard before Joe slammed the door closed again. The alarm continued to blare.

"Let's get out of here!" Frank shouted.

The three of them ran to the door and jerked it open. A security guard ran at them, his revolver drawn.

"Freeze!" he shouted.

Joe, Frank, and Eric Wright stopped where they were and raised their hands over their heads. The muzzle of the .38 swung back and forth to cover all three of them. Suddenly Frank noticed the insignia on the guard's green jacket. Now he recognized both the guard and the jacket. It was the same man who had tried to chain-saw Adam's maple trees.

Chapter

15

THE SECURITY GUARD reached for the two-way radio strapped to his belt and called in a report. Within minutes, Chief O'Brien came speeding up to the plant entrance. He looked furious.

"I'm surprised at you boys," he said. "There's no excuse for breaking the law. And you, Eric Wright, a trusted state employee—what made you risk your career like this?"

Eric hung his head and didn't answer.

"I'm going to have to take you in," O'Brien continued. "Let's go."

The guard asked, "You want me to come along and keep them covered?"

"That won't be necessary," the chief said coolly.

"You going to put the cuffs on them?" the guard added, leering at the Hardys.

"No," O'Brien snapped. "And stop waving that pistol around."

Outside, the three prisoners climbed in the backseat of the cruiser. O'Brien shut the door and went around to the driver's seat. As he pulled away, Frank looked back at the guard. The smirk on his face said clearly that he remembered the Hardys from the encounter in Karl's sugar bush.

The Waterboro Police Station was in the basement of the town hall. O'Brien's assistant wrote up a report on Frank, Joe, and Eric, took their fingerprints, and snapped instant photos of them.

"I'm sorry to do this, boys," Chief O'Brien said. "But I've got no choice. You were breaking and entering," He cocked an eyebrow at Frank. "You going to tell me what you were doing inside Gagnon's plant?"

"We were investigating—" Joe rushed in to explain, but Frank cut him off.

"We're just working theories at this point, Chief," he said quickly. "If there's something the police should be aware of, you'll be the first to know."

"Okay," said the chief with a sigh. "I know better than to question you further. Just promise you'll keep me informed."

Frank held up a few fingers as if he were taking a pledge. "You have my word."

O'Brien's assistant led the three of them back to the one cell and shut them in.

A short time later, O'Brien let Frank out to telephone Adam to come post bail.

When he heard where the Hardys were, Adam shouted, "I'll be right down."

While they waited for Adam, Eric paced up and down inside the tiny cell. "I can't believe I've been arrested," he said. "I don't know how I'm ever going to explain this to my boss."

"I know what you mean," Joe agreed solemnly. "Our dad's not going to be too happy about it either."

"Don't worry," Frank told both of them. "I have a feeling that if we can figure out what's going on at Gagnon's factory, he's not going to be in any position to press charges."

Joe dropped down on the rickety chair that sat in the corner of the cell. "That guard was definitely one of the guys trying to saw down Karl's maples," he said. "I bet Gagnon put him and the others up to it."

"But why would Gagnon do that?" Eric asked.

"Gagnon developed this laboratory syrup, and now he's got to convince people to buy it," Frank explained. "If he can scare real sugarers like Adam and Karl into quitting the business at the

135

same time he's scaring customers with the threat of poisoning, he's got it made."

"He's responsible for the poisoning, too, then?" asked Eric.

"Got to be," Frank replied. "He's got the motive—money. He probably has the means—altered maple genes. And opportunity, too. That sprayer Joe found— The intruder we saw up in Karl's sugar bush had one just like it on his back."

"He must have been spraying something on the trees," Joe added. "Want to bet what it is?"

Frank stepped the four paces to the back wall and leaned against it. "What gets me is that Adam and Karl must have a couple hundred trees apiece. Could Gagnon do that to all of them?"

"Maybe he had help," Eric said. "Even if he didn't, he probably wouldn't have to infect every single tree. Let's say he infected half of them. Sooner or later the altered sap would mix with the rest of the sap in the holding tanks and evaporator and produce the same effects when it was boiled down into syrup."

Eric paused, then continued. "Chances are, he's been at this awhile. It would take some time for the altered genes to work their way into the tree cells, override the original system, and start producing the dangerous sap."

Frank said, "I really think we've broken this

case wide open. But now what we need is hard evidence."

"What we need now," Joe reminded him, "is to get out of the slammer."

They fell silent as Chief O'Brien appeared in the corridor outside the cell. "You've got a visitor," he announced.

"That was fast," Joe started to say.

But the visitor wasn't Adam coming to pick them up. It was Nick Unger.

"Give a shout when you're done," O'Brien said, and left.

Nick stood outside the iron bars and looked at Frank, Joe, and Eric, who stared back at him. "I guess you didn't expect to see me here," he said.

"That's true," Frank replied, and waited for an explanation.

Nervous and unsure, Nick jingled the coins in his pocket. He started to say something, stopped, and started again. "News travels fast in small towns," he said. "You're trying to find out who's behind this poisoning thing, and you think it's me. Am I right?"

"You're not far from wrong," Joe responded.

"I swear I didn't have a thing to do with it," Unger said. Frank saw tiny beads of sweat along his hairline.

"You know that watch of mine?" Unger continued. "Somebody put it there in French's wood-lot. And I think I know who. Jud Gagnon. He dropped by my office a couple of weeks ago. I went off to wash my hands, and I'm pretty sure I left my watch on my desk. But that evening, I couldn't find it anywhere."

"Why would Gagnon steal your watch?" Joe asked. "It has your initials engraved on it."

"That's the point," Unger said eagerly. "He was already planning to set me up. He planted my watch, then called me to send me up to French's property, just in time to get caught. Don't you see—I was framed!"

"And you think it was Gagnon who called you?" Frank asked.

Unger nodded. "It had to be. It's the only way that makes any sense."

Frank continued, "But you didn't recognize his voice?"

Unger shrugged. "It didn't sound like anyone I know. But that's not hard to manage. I saw an ad in the paper the other day for a gadget that makes your voice sound like anything you want."

"Why should we believe you?" Frank demanded. "Maybe you and Gagnon were working together on this, and now you're trying to bail out."

"No!" Unger said, his eyes wide with fear. "You've got to believe me."

Chief O'Brien reappeared. "Time's up, Nick," he said.

The real estate agent gave Frank and Joe a

pleading look, then turned and left without another word.

A little while later, Adam arrived, with Karl, Callie, and Vanessa in tow. He posted bail for the Hardys and Eric. Outside on the street, Eric told everyone he had had enough of Waterboro to last him a few years, and left for Concord.

Adam turned to the Hardys. "Well, you've had a pretty adventurous day. Ready to turn in?"

Frank shook his head. "We're close to solving this case, Adam." He quickly filled in the others on what they'd learned at the lab. "We can't quit now."

"I had an inkling you'd say that," Adam said with a smile. "What's next, then?"

"Hard, cold evidence," Joe said. "That's what we need."

"And we know where to find it," Frank added. "In Gagnon's lab."

Joe met his eye. "That canister in the freezer?"

Frank nodded. "It had a label that read Biohazard," he explained to the others. "I'm guessing that it contains the genetically engineered maple genes Gagnon sprayed on the trees to make them produce deadly sap. If we can get it, we'll have the proof we need."

"Talk to Chief O'Brien," Callie urged him. "Tell him everything you know and let him take it from here."

"I wish we could." Frank shook his head. "I

promised O'Brien we'd keep him informed. But if we let him go after the canister, he'll have to go to a judge for a search warrant. And Gagnon already knows we're onto him. He'll destroy or hide the evidence before the chief has a chance to get to his factory."

"If you're going back to Gagnon's plant, we're coming, too," Vanessa declared.

Frank thought fast. Eric Wright had already gotten arrested because of Frank and Joe; there was no way Frank was going to let anyone else risk getting into trouble.

"I don't think that's a good idea," he said. "The more people who come, the greater the chance we'll get caught. And if we *do* get caught, we're going to need friends around to bail us out."

"So just give us a lift to Gagnon's factory, where we left the van," Joe added.

"All right," Vanessa responded reluctantly. "But if you're not back at the farm in two hours, I'm going to come looking for you. That's a promise."

"We'll all come looking for you," Karl added. "And we won't be any too quiet about it, either."

The guys had Karl drop them off about a hundred yards from Gagnon's Gold factory. From the cover of an alley, the two brothers watched for five minutes. The plant was dark, apparently deserted.

"That's one good thing," Joe remarked in a low voice. "It'll never occur to anyone that we'd be idiotic enough to come back so soon."

Before reentering the plant, they stopped by the van, still parked a little way down the street. There they armed themselves with a steel pry bar, a pair of fence cutters, a set of lockpicks, and two miniature flashlights.

The door they had used before was locked. They moved along the side of the building, checking out the windows. The fourth one opened onto a rest room. Joe forced the lock, raised the window, climbed in, and then gave Frank a hand.

They opened the rest room door a crack and listened. Silence. Frank tapped Joe's arm and motioned him down the hall. They crept single file to the door to the laboratory. It was locked, but after a few minutes of work, Frank managed to pick the lock.

He slipped inside, with Joe close behind him, and shut the door without a sound. Then Frank led the way across the room, between the rows of high-tech electronic equipment, to the freezer unit.

Joe knew what to do. He got down on his knees and felt around the back of the freezer for the alarm wire. Holding his breath, he snipped it. To his relief, nothing happened. Fortunately, the alarm wasn't on a fail-safe circuit that would set off the alarm whenever anything interfered with the system. He looked at Frank and gave him a thumbs-up sign.

Frank grasped the handle of the freezer door and turned it. It didn't budge. Was it locked? He shone his light on the area around the handle, without finding a keyhole. Taking the handle again, he gave it a good, hard jerk. The door sprang open. His light fell directly on the canister labeled Biohazard.

"We've got it," Frank whispered triumphantly, grabbing the crucial evidence. "Let's get out of here!"

They were halfway to the door when it crashed open. The rows of lights in the ceiling suddenly went on.

Blinded by the glare, Frank shielded his eyes. Then he looked in the direction of the door.

Standing in the center of the doorway, blocking their escape route, was Jud Gagnon. His fists were clenched, and his face was a red mask of fury.

Chapter

16

"WHAT ARE YOU DOING HERE?" Gagnon shouted. Then he spotted the canister in Joe's hands, and the blood drained from his face. "That's mine!" he exclaimed. "Give it to me."

"No," Frank said, keeping one eye on Joe, who was clutching the canister and backing away. "This is the evidence we've been looking for. It's going to put you away for a long, long time."

"Do you know who I am?" Gagnon demanded in a menacing tone. "I own this plant. I'm a well-known businessman. I give jobs to people around here and bring income to the town. Who will people believe—me, or a couple of kids from who knows where? They'll laugh right in your faces."

"Nobody around here is in the mood to laugh at poisoning," Frank said. "Once they find out what you've been doing, you'll be glad to have the protection of a nice, secure jail."

Joe added, "We know why you're here. Just like us, you wanted to get this canister. But you wanted to destroy it, to hide the evidence—didn't you?"

"That's ridiculous," Gagnon declared. "We have some very sensitive experiments going on here. I came by to check on them."

"That's a lie," Frank snapped.

Gagnon straightened up and took a deep breath. "Look, I can have you arrested again. This time it would be for burglary, a much more serious crime than breaking and entering. A conviction like that would ruin your lives." He stared at them, as if letting them think it over for a few minutes.

Then his steely gaze softened. "The fact is, this is a sensitive time for my business. I'm just launching my new product, Gagnon's Gold syrup. The last thing I need is bad publicity. So here's the deal, boys. You hand over that canister and leave my plant now, and you'll never hear another word about this. No charges, no criminal record, no time in jail for either offense. What do you say?"

He took a step toward Joe and held out his

hand. Joe took a matching step backward. Gagnon's smile faded.

"Listen, kid," he growled. "Can you read? What does it say on the side of that container?"

Joe gave him a tight smile. " 'Biohazard,' " he replied, taking another step backward.

"Exactly," Gagnon said. "That stuff is very, very dangerous. Now, hand it over, before you get hurt."

Joe shook his head.

"What do you mean, no?" Gagnon demanded.

"We're not going to hand it over," Frank explained. "We're going to give it to the authorities. And besides, I doubt this substance is dangerous to us. We're not maple trees."

Gagnon snarled, then made a sudden lunge for Joe.

"Joe!" Frank called. "Single wing!"

That was all Joe needed to hear. While Frank charged at Gagnon from the left, he tucked the canister under his arm and went wide to the right, around a lab table cluttered with test tubes and equipment. Gagnon, faked out by the Hardys' abrupt movements, hesitated. An instant later, Frank tackled him, while Joe made a run for the doorway.

"No, you don't!" The infuriated Gagnon brought his knee up, catching Frank under the chin, and whirled around to grab the sleeve of Joe's jacket.

Caught off balance, Joe stumbled toward Gagnon. He felt himself losing his grip on the canister. As he stumbled to the floor, he shouted, "Frank!" and made an underhand lateral pass.

Frank scooped up the canister and dodged around an equipment cart. At the same time, Joe grabbed a stool, tipped it on its side, and thrust it toward Gagnon's legs. Gagnon tripped and fell forward over it. But somehow he found the agility to reach out and grab Frank's ankle.

Desperately Frank leaped over Gagnon. He could feel his grip on the canister slipping. It went flying across the room and crashed to the floor, rolling under one of the lab tables.

"Get it, Joe!" Frank yelled. He threw himself down on top of Gagnon. But Gagnon rolled aside and jumped up.

Joe scooped up the canister and again made a dash for the door. Gagnon charged after him. But instead of grabbing him, he reached for a long-handled fire ax hanging on the wall. He ripped the ax from its safety latch and gripped it with both fists.

"Joe!" Frank shouted. "Watch out!"

Gagnon cocked the gleaming ax like a baseball bat and swung it at Joe. Joe fell to his hands and knees, then scrambled for the shelter of the nearest lab table.

Frank jumped to his feet. He grabbed a stool and held it up between him and Gagnon like a lion tamer. As Frank advanced, Gagnon's eyes flicked from him to Joe, who was crawling toward the door.

With Frank only two feet away, and coming closer every second, Gagnon was forced to turn all his attention to Frank. He swung the ax high into the air, then chopped downward, straight at Frank's face. Frank threw the stool at his opponent, then dodged to one side. The ax struck the stool, splintering it.

Gagnon yanked the ax out, then scanned the room for Joe. He spotted him, on his feet now, near the door. With a terrifying cry, Gagnon struck out with mad force. He hurled the ax through the air toward Joe. Joe ducked, and the blade tore through the Sheetrock wall, slicing it as if it were paper.

"Hie-yaa!" Frank launched himself into a flying kick that connected with Gagnon's midsection. Gasping for breath, Gagnon bent double, holding his arms to his stomach.

"Run, Joe!" Frank shouted. "I'll deal with him!"

Joe dashed toward the door. But suddenly Chief O'Brien and his assistant were standing there, service revolvers at the ready.

"Freeze!" O'Brien growled. "Nobody move!"

"Chief!" Gagnon panted. "Thank goodness you're here. I caught these two hoodlums trying to burglarize my plant. They would have killed me if you hadn't come."

Frank met Joe's eye. Would O'Brien fall for Gagnon's lies?

Then Callie and Vanessa walked in.

"We borrowed Uncle Adam's old pickup and sneaked into town," Callie said. "Once we told Chief O'Brien what we suspected, he agreed to come over here and check it out."

Joe held up the canister, then handed it to the police chief. "Here," he said. "This is the proof that Jud Gagnon is behind the poisoning."

O'Brien glared at Gagnon. "I'm going to read you your rights, Mr. Gagnon." Then he pulled a card from his pocket and read from it.

Gagnon listened, an angry scowl on his face.

Then the chief held up the canister. "What's in this thing?"

Gagnon stared blankly. Then, in a voice that could hardly be heard, he said, "Molecularly altered maple tree genes."

Frank glanced at Joe. They were right! Gagnon had been using altered genes to damage the trees.

O'Brien still looked confused.

"Just tell Mr. Maas what Gagnon said," Frank suggested with a grin. "He'll understand."

Turning to Gagnon, Frank asked, "You sabotaged Adam's and Karl's sugar bushes with that stuff, didn't you?"

"It was an experiment," Gagnon said. "I had to show that it could be done."

"You showed you could poison a bunch of people," Joe said angrily.

"Was your whole lab team involved?" Frank asked.

Gagnon shrugged. "They did what they were told to do," he said. "Nobody asked exactly what it was all for. They knew that if they did, they'd be out of a job."

"And that security guard," Joe probed. "You ordered him to cut down Karl's maples, didn't you?"

"Uh . . . that was a matter of public safety," Gagnon fumbled. "The sap of those trees was dangerous."

Frank stared at him in disbelief. "Of course it was," he exclaimed. "You made it that way!"

Joe asked, "Was that one of your employees who went to the town offices and asked those sneaky questions about a new development? You were hoping to throw suspicion on Nick Unger, right?"

Gagnon smiled this time, as if he thought that had been a clever move on his part. "He was a guy I hired from a temp agency in Concord," he explained.

"You stole Unger's watch for the same purpose, didn't you?" Frank continued. "To throw the blame on him for your crimes."

"Listen, Nick Unger's no angel," Gagnon protested. "He's up to all kinds of little schemes."

"But they don't involve poisoning people, do they?" Frank pointed out. "You were ready to stop at nothing, weren't you? Framing Nick, throwing a brick through our window ... By the way, who told you which room we were in?"

"Nobody," Gagnon said sullenly. "I waited outside to see which window shade you pulled down."

"But that wasn't as bad as blowing up Karl's sugarhouse," Joe continued. "You could have killed him and Adam both, you know that?"

The expression on Gagnon's face said that he couldn't have cared less.

"That's enough," Chief O'Brien intervened. "I'll get a formal statement from him down at the station." He glanced at Frank and Joe. "And a guarantee that the breaking and entering charges against you will be dropped. Come on, Gagnon. I'm going to have to put these cuffs on you."

O'Brien led Gagnon to his cruiser and put him in the backseat, then drove off, leaving Joe, Frank, Callie, and Vanessa standing in the factory parking lot.

Frank gave a big yawn, then said, "Let's get back to the house. I'm totally whipped."

They had barely reached the house when the first carload of newspeople arrived. The others weren't far behind. All of them wanted interviews for their morning papers, news programs, and talk shows. It was well after midnight when Adam finally chased the last of them away.

The next morning, Karl came over bright and early. On his face was a big smile. "I've got to hand it to you," he told Frank and Joe. "Who would've thought that two young pups—who know nothing about sugaring—would be the ones to stop Jud Gagnon from ruining our business?"

"Yup." Adam gave a crooked grin. "And now that the mystery's solved, these two can do some *real* work around here to earn their keep."

Everyone laughed.

Adam made coffee and they all trooped into the living room to read the papers and watch the news on TV. In all the stories, O'Brien gave Joe and Frank full credit for breaking the case and revealing Gagnon's scheme. Even Connie Page praised the Hardys and called Gagnon a master criminal who'd tried to ruin the lives of two innocent citizens—Adam Shaw and Karl French. While she said it, Frank noticed her face puckering up, as if she were sucking on a lemon.

"You know what else I heard?" Karl declared. "Nick Unger is leaving town. I guess he figured out that folks around here won't have anything to do with him now that this secret plan to build a big resort on our land is out in the open."

"And good riddance," Adam grumbled. "The old dirt bag."

The phone rang. Adam picked up the receiver and talked quietly for a few moments. Then he hung up and turned to the others. "That was Bob," he said. "He heard about what happened, and he's on his way back to take up his old job."

Only then did Adam smile.

"When I spoke to Eric Wright this morning," Frank began, "he said your trees will be back to normal next year. Does that mean you two will go on sugaring?"

"No two-bit jug-head Gagnon is going to stop me," Adam said. "But I've been thinking that first I might help Karl rebuild his sugarhouse."

Karl kept a straight face as he said, "And I've been thinking that maybe we ought to merge our operations. How do you like French and Shaw Farms Pure Maple Syrup?"

"It's catchy," Adam admitted. "But why not *Shaw* and French Farms Syrup?"

Everybody laughed.

"Well," Joe said. "This is one case where we couldn't see the forest for the trees."

Frank groaned. "That was pretty lame, bro." He turned to Adam. "But now that we've solved this case, can we please go skiing?"

Frank and Joe's next case:

The Hardy boys have signed on as stagehands for Legerdemania—the annual extravaganza showcasing the world's master magicians. But this year's spectacular proves to be a killer. Gideon the Great's assistant Miranda was supposed to do a vanishing act. Instead she ends up dead . . . and the murderer disappears! The competition onstage is fierce, and Frank and Joe soon discover that just about every magician has a motive for murder. And determined to avoid exposure, the real killer is more than willing to perform an encore. The Hardys will have to come up with some hocus-pocus of their own, or they might end up victims of the dirtiest, deadliest trick of all . . . in *Murder by Magic,* Case #98 in The Hardy Boys Casefiles™.